Blackberry Way

Also by Walter G. Klimczak

Falling in the Garden

This Place Only

My Forgotten Life

Praise for *Falling in the Garden*

*"...a magical miracle... involving time travel
and alternate dimensions. The author's touch is light,
keeping the (pseudo)scientific explanations to a
minimum while holding in the foreground Michael's
insatiable thirst for discovery and his budding feelings
of adolescent romance. The story is... tightly plotted,
with the mystery building quickly and smoothly. (An)
enjoyable journey. The best kind of science fiction: The
science sows the seeds, but the story grows the
garden."*

–Kirkus Reviews

Blackberry Way

Walter G. Klimczak

Autumn Harbor Press, Ltd.
Atlanta, Georgia

Blackberry
Way

Autumn Harbor Press, Ltd.
Atlanta, Georgia

FIRST EDITION

July 2007

ISBN 978-0-6151-4636-2

*For more information about Autumn Harbor books,
please visit our website @ www.autumnharbor.com*

This book is dedicated to my mother, Karen.

This book is also dedicated to
Ben, Lily, Joe and Carrie Tompkins.
They were my second family during a very special
time in my life and for this I am truly grateful.

"Those who dream by day are cognizant of many things which escape those who dream only by night."

Edgar Allan Poe

"The communication of the dead is tongued with fire beyond the language of the living."

T. S. Eliot

darkness is the soul
forever creeping southward
in the form of rain

This haiku was found scribbled on the back cover of
the last of Michael Dorigan's three journals.

forward

My name is Theresa Kincaid and I am a retired investigative reporter, but this story is not about me. I moved from New York State to South Carolina a little over a year ago. Two months after I settled into my new home, I made the most remarkable discovery. In a recess hidden behind some wall boards in the hallway linen closet, I found three notebooks. They contain the incredible account you now hold in your hands. Some minor editing was (I believe) necessary to tame a somewhat emotional, stream-of-conscious narrative, though I have done my best to leave the writing in its original form.

I now offer you the story of Michael Dorigan.

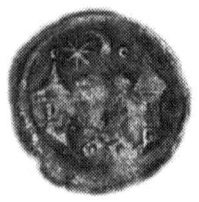

one

"Michael? Could you come here a minute?"

I'd been listening to this for over an hour, but didn't move. Didn't say a word. The typewriter sat humming before me with a blank sheet in the rollers. The door to the study was closed, but I could still hear her clearly from somewhere upstairs.

"Michael?"

The study had no windows, but the sound of rain somehow pushed its way through. Pounding on the roof. Filling me with static. Never letting up.

I turned to look at the clock on the bookshelf.

Three-fifteen. Jeni should be—

"Daddy! I'm home!" The front door banged shut.

"Can I have something before dinner?" she called. "I forgot my lunch and all I had was half of Ellie Kasner's cheese sandwich!"

Just the paper before me.

Blank; my mind.

"Daddy?"

I didn't answer. Just the mention of food made my stomach churn. I hadn't eaten in... how many days was it? Moira called down:

"Michael? Could you make Jeni something quick? There's some chicken salad in the fridge. Second shelf."

Chicken salad.

I typed, **CHICKEN SALAD**

Stared at the words.

It was an old typewriter. I bought it second-hand my first year in high school. Rusted in places, a hell of a load to carry, but still a God-honest typewriter. I fell in love with it immediately, and it was on this machine that I wrote my first novel.

I typed, **YOUR FIRST BOOK WAS CRAP!**

And from the kitchen, Jeni screamed, "Your first book was crap!" She was in the third grade and had never before used such language, though I'm sure she heard her share of it. Jeni always gave me a special sort of inspiration when I wrote. Although I had never directly based a character on her, my strongest and most easy-going ones were those to whom I attributed her total and complete openness. She breathed life into my writing. As did Moira, though Moira helped in other more immediate ways. She was there for me when I found myself lost between the words, searching for an answer. She gave me the support I needed at the end of a book, when I thought that it *was* a piece of shit, wanting to toss the pages into the fireplace one by one. In that darkened void where I swam to find meaning, she never turned out her light.

I typed, **I'LL NEVER STOP LOVING YOU**

I listened: footsteps above me. Moving over me. Down the stairs, the hallway. Just outside the study door. And my wife said, just above a whisper, "I'll never stop loving you."

Outside, the rain was an endless disturbance of white

noise, filling and completing with stark emptiness.

In the corner of the room sat a lounge chair, a place where Moira read my chapters, the good and the ugly. Two weeks ago she had sat there reading a short story, one I'd written specifically for her. When she finished, she looked over at me and I'll never forget the look on her face. She said nothing, walked over to me, took my hands in hers...

What good could possibly come from such stupid games? The problem was that I was good at it. I made my life playing out fictional worlds on paper. It was only now that I had to stop, at least for a while. It would be the only thing to keep me from going insane.

A knock at the study door. Moira:

"Michael, honey? Is everything alright?" And I could hear Jeni, too, asking her mother something just under her breath.

I typed, **STOP**

And it did. All of it.

I turned the typewriter off and rolled the paper out and crushed it into a tight ball, squeezing it in my hand. The only light that filled the room came from a small fisherman's lamp on my desk, casting a warm, buttery glow on everything. I left it on and moved toward the door. I could no longer hear Moira. Or Jeni. It was as I had asked.

Dropping the wadded paper, I reached out to the cold knob and held onto it a few seconds so the metal might turn warm in my hand. It didn't. Still cold, I finally turned it, pulled the door open and walked down the hallway. Before me, in an overwhelming, near-silent flood coursed the rain on the kitchen windows. Walking further in, it seemed as if I were standing still (a fixed point) and the house moved around me. I then found myself in the center of the kitchen, staring at the refrigerator.

There's some chicken salad in the fridge! Second shelf!

Stuck to the refrigerator door with magnets shaped like vegetables were masterpieces in crayon and watercolor created by Jeni. There was a calendar as well.

Squinting, I stared at the tiny box that was July eleventh, two days from now. In Moira's handwriting:

Fifth Annual
Dorigan Picnic

But there would be no picnic, isn't that right Mr. Mike?

That's what my father had called me when I was a child. *Mr. Mike.* Dad was a practical man. In raising both my sister and I he balked at such things as going to the playground, playing hide-and-seek and unrestrained laughter, things our mother only encouraged. He believed in responsibility, indoctrinating the two of us every chance he could. So, my sister was referred to as Miss Rose and I as—

You're playing with some dangerous thoughts, Mr. Mike. Messing around with ideas that'll haunt you if you don't let them go. Forget the calendar. Forget it all.

I knew I had to. The picnic would never happen because they're dead. Both of them.

There, I've said it. They're dead.

Just then, my legs decided not to work. Like weakening ice on an early-spring pond, they melted and left me stranded.

There was nothing more I could do but sit there and accept.

The light that fell through the windows, warped by the pulsing of rain, caused phantom, jelly-like waves to appear on the linoleum. I existed inside this shifty portrait as an island.

There wasn't a hint of thunder in the distance. No sound but for the rain. And, somewhere deep within it, an all-consuming silence.

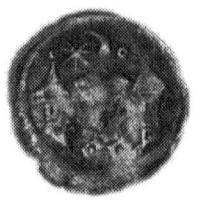

two

I told myself Sunday would be the day, but it wasn't quite so easy. Its one thing to sell a house and buy another (my good friend, Peter Fausta, knew people in real-estate and took care of all that for me), but it's another to actually move. To pack. Yet I knew this was something I needed to do. Every night was horrible, reaching for Moira's warm shoulder and finding her side of the bed cool. Longing to hold her in my arms, to be held in hers, and letting it all build up inside. Such a significant part of me had been irrevocably ripped away, stolen without even the slightest hope of return. And there was no thief except the night, and the cruelty of the dreaming mind that launched a thousand painful ways of telling me, "So sorry, Michael, it's better to have loved and lost..."

  I couldn't shut it off, couldn't pull the cord. At its mercy, forever beneath a world of grey that filled each empty moment with weightiness, numbing liquids.

Which I helplessly drank.

Packing. Our room first. Moira and I had shared the walk-in closet, so it was impossible to avoid her dresses, each the embodiment and convocation of the past. A yellow summer dress: this past spring at Lake Tahoe—our summer house. The week Jeni first learned to swim. Moira's soft, brown hair streaked delicately with golden highlights. She'd accumulated two weeks vacation-time from the clinic and devoted every hour to our family. Her vacations were usually reserved for day-trips to her parents, which was fine since Jeni and I had her on the evenings and weekends. I spent most of my time at home writing, so I saw Jeni most often. I at first thought that once Moira started working again, six months after Jeni was born, both mother and daughter would not see each other as often as they should. I was happily proven wrong, as Moira spent more time—with Jeni and with me— than it seemed she had.

A soft, green jumpsuit: last Easter at my parent's house in New Hampshire. Mom and Dad absolutely adored Jeni, and our daughter would never return home without having unearthed at least one of my sister Rose's old dresses from Mom's attic. Though my father didn't impress the same qualities on Jeni as he did Rose and I so many years ago, some words of wisdom did brush off. This was easily seen in regard to dress-up. Jeni had always taken dress-up seriously, kept all her play clothes neatly hung or folded in boxes beneath her bed. Dad's philosophy had softened over time, reduced to: well, if you're going to play, you can at least do it in an orderly fashion. It was still near impossible recalling the way he'd been, in all his military regimen, when he scooped up our daughter and called her Jeni-bean.

There are two pictures hanging in the down-stairs hallway: one of Rose wearing a pink party dress and the other of Jeni wearing the very same outfit twenty-three years later. Virtual twins. And the green evening dress I now held in my hands where once I held Moira in the same fabric, not two or three days ago. Time, now, held no texture—merely an emptiness that is space where thoughts and memories float freely and without order.

All her dresses, on the bed.

I looked past the curtains, out into the morning and found the sky a heavy grey blanket, so heavy it slouched, but nothing became of it. *Rain*, I willed it. *Rain and fill the air; give it substance*, but there was nothing. I piled the remainder of her clothes with the dresses and the bed-covers were no longer visible. A cloth mountain that watched me with indifference, didn't speak, did not accuse.

But there was more—Moira's jewelry. Other things. Photo-albums. Pictures going back over the years, before Jeni was born to when Moira and I first met. I knew each picture by heart, but couldn't find the strength to open even one of the books. Didn't know how I would react, which truly frightened me.

I left the mountain and brought the bound photos downstairs, into the living room where Pete had left me five or six dozen folded cardboard boxes. I set the albums down onto the coffee table and ran back upstairs, sweat causing an old University of Maine t-shirt I wore to cling like paste to my back. Past our bedroom door to Jeni's room, and then to a place somewhere between where the cold, hidden moon shone enough pale light for me to see her standing there in her Strawberry Shortcake pajamas. It was Christmas Eve again and her eyes were wide and her words came out in a gasp:

"Did you hear that?"

"Hear what, sweetie?"

"The noise on the roof! Do you think it's... him?"

Moira and I soon tucked her in, whispering secrets of Santa's visit, and she brushed her lips against my cheek, whispering, "I love you, Daddy." I stood there in the doorway, my entire body shaking. Christmas Eve was nothing more than a mote of dust. Each moment I looked back sent forward sharp and painful daggers. I couldn't move. Could not pass through her doorway. Her bed was still unmade and one of her pillows rested on the floor, half-obscuring a tattered, though well-loved doll. My mother had made it for her from the same sheet that covered my bed when I was a child. And then, without warning, I was allowed to pass, sailing into the room on a coaxing wind.

Kneeling at the foot of her bed, I stretched my arms out over the blankets, pulled the sheets back then carefully tucked the remaining fabric under the top mattress. Jeni always made her bed in the morning. Never forgot. Why had it slipped her mind this last time?

"Sing for me?" she sometimes asked before bed, and I'd oblige with an off-key rendition of 'Who's Afraid of the Big Bad Wolf' and she would laugh. How I loved to make her laugh. Laughter I would never again hear.

I picked up her pillow and followed the parade of Disney characters that danced across it. The bedspread, too, held host to Mickey, Minnie and friends. My knee kicked at something beneath the bed and I reached under to discover one of her boxes of play clothes.

Running out into the hallway, blinded by a stinging in my eyes, I again found myself in my own bedroom with the clothes mountain and dug into it, searching for Moira's pillow. It seemed for awful seconds that it was gone, swallowed by the heartless mound, but I found it. Wrapped my arms tightly around it. Squeezed it, spinning slowly in circles, eyes closed. Brought it to my face and breathed deeply and she was both with me and no where at all. Was it possible to measure the miles we'd been thrown apart? Farther than billions of light years. It seemed unimaginable that any two things could be more distant. At the same time I wanted to tear the pillow apart and never let it go. Moira's scent was still with it, with me.

Spinning. Turning. Unending.

three

That afternoon I did the worst thing possible and made the decision not to attend the funeral. I know I should have gone. Instead, I locked the doors and closed the curtains.

There was knocking on the front, back and side doors. I didn't answer, but knew who they were. My parents. Moira's parents. Rose. Probably Pete.

I sat quietly in the living room as yesterday's rain warped forcefully into a storm and listened to Moira's old records. I'd been collecting CDs for the past few years, but she preferred her scratchy LPs. I sat there on the floor beside the stereo, floating through The Eagles, Renaissance and The Electric Light Orchestra. Staring at the still unopened pile of photo albums, I ignored the thunder that boomed like fists of angry demons on my safe, yet temporary sanctuary.

It was then that I learned how to push the pain (that unbearable, unrelenting single-minded pain) deep inside. I couldn't bottle it all, though, and was left to sip hesitantly at what remained. I knew avoidance was wrong, but could think of no alternative. Did not want to think. Did not want to feel.

Welcoming the spiral fall of music, spinning darkly, I was carried off...

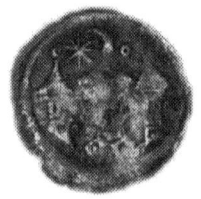

four

A move from Upstate New York to the countryside of the South, Pete had said, was a change I desperately needed. Though a practicing psychologist, he'd never before given Moira and I professional advice. Sure, I'd talked with him about problems, but never in a doctor-patient context. Now, however, he took my situation (my *condition*) seriously. I answered all his questions without hesitation, giving him what he wanted not because I thought he could help, but because I really didn't care one way or the other. When he finally approached me with the idea of moving, I only nodded, wanting to get it over with. He seemed, at first, surprised by my immediate cooperation, and was almost hesitant about my wanting to do things as quickly as possible. Then, for hours it seemed (though surely it was only minutes) silence parted us.

We sat at the kitchen table with Kahlúa-spiked coffee and blank stares. Before me sat a small stack of papers, each waiting to be signed.

And a pen; upon its side were the words: *MCWHORTER FUNERAL HOME.* Though I knew Pete had no intention of wanting me to sign with that specific pen, I pretended not to notice. I didn't pick it up.

"—you'd drive," he finished, and I forced myself to look up at attention, unaware that he'd actually spoken.

"I'm sorry." I murmured, catching only a fraction of what he'd said.

"To Sweetwater. I still wish you'd consider driving. You know I think you're moving kind of fast with this and I really think it would be best if you had a little more time to think—"

"Think?" I interrupted, "About what?" And my challenge stood. I didn't mean to put him so tightly on the spot, but did so anyway. He sprung back quicker than I expected, his voice almost strident.

"Think, Michael. Think about what you're going to do."

"Hold on a second, I don't... What do you *think* I'll be doing? I'm still a writer."

"I don't mean to bring you down, but you're not yet America's #1 best-selling author. You've been successful, granted, but how is everything that's happened going to affect your career?"

I snatched up the pen and rose from the table, tapping the plastic casing on different surfaces: the kitchen counter, the top of a chair, the window frame.

"I don't believe this," I said, and it was strange! Moira was my number one support base when it came to my writing, Dorothy Midland (my agent) second; running close third was Pete.

"Look," his voice softened. Trying a different approach? "All I'm saying is that you should wait a few more days before getting settled down in Sweetwater."

"Why? Is something wrong with the house?"

"No, the house is fine," and his smile faded.

"What then?"

"Nothing," he whispered, looking out the window, focusing intently on some object. "You used to trust me on things like this, Mike. Why do you keep doubting me?"

"Why all of the sudden are you putting down my writing?"

He looked straight at me. "I'm not putting it down, I'm just... damn, I can only imagine what you're going through. Moira was like a sister to me, and Jeni..."

Was it my turn to say something? Did it matter? I was already feeling feverish at his mention of them. It didn't seem right for anyone else to say their names. I didn't know why I felt this way, but it nagged incessantly. I allowed enough silence to pass before speaking.

"My airline ticket is for tomorrow."

"Eleven fifty-five. You're on a Delta flight out of Stewart."

I was now tossing the pen from one hand to the other, rolling it between my palms, ready to snap it in two if the urge so presented itself. Why the hell had he gone and checked my flight schedule?

"I don't know what you're up to, Pete, but—"

"I'm not *up* to anything. Trust me on this, okay?"

"So... you want me to drive down there instead of a quick and easy flight." I stated this. It was not a question.

He only stared, eyeing me intently. His face acknowledged what I had said. I was in no mood to continue. Did not want to hear him say their names again.

Grip loosening on the pen, I sat down once more and took the papers, began to sign them. I don't know how he did it, but he always had a way of getting in the last word, even when he didn't say a thing. When we were younger, he saw everything as a contest. He hadn't changed. Even in this simple exchange, where no contest was evident, Pete sat there victorious, a certain sureness in his eyes—the bold way he held himself. It would have made anyone else angry, even furious, but I'd learned how to deal with it.

"I'm having problems with my car," I mumbled.

Pete jumped right in with, "I reserved you a rental after the..."

Funeral?

"...yesterday afternoon."

I think I smiled, nearly laughed. His expression didn't change. Still the winner in a game without rules. This entire scene was completely insane. He was playing me, though I didn't know why; I allowed it to happen regardless. Signing the last page, I clicked the pen off and set it on top of the papers. As slowly as I could manage, I walked toward the bay windows overlooking the back yard: Jeni's swing set, both swings rocking slow-motion in the wind. A blue Frisbee lying top-down in the grass, a rippling, rain-water sea collected inside it, courtesy of last night's storm. The sky was still overcast. Perhaps the rain had not yet said farewell.

"I'll give you that," I said with a sigh, not turning around, not wanting to look at him, mad at him, mad at myself for being even slightly angry. I stared out into the miniature, Frisbee ocean, so tired. "You've taken care of everything."

It was all so quiet. I could barely tell that Pete was there behind me. Could hardly tell that *I* was there.

An empty house, as soon it would be.

five

I put only those things I needed in the trunk. The rental car had that 'new car' smell and it nearly made me sick. I'd have kept the windows open, but the rain came down harder than it had all week. The wipers threw off only half of the downpour, but the roads weren't too terrible and I made it well enough.

Still, I couldn't stop thinking: why was Pete acting so strange? He even offered to finish my packing (and I almost told him no!) but accepted because I knew I'd never get it done myself, never finish, just drown in the memories; in those waters I'd forgotten how to swim.

So why was it that the rain kept falling and seemed to go nowhere? Sure, they say it eventually made its way back to the sea, to lakes and ponds where again it would take to the atmosphere. I wasn't entirely sure of that. Of course, this scenario probably holds true for *most* kinds of rain, but not all.

Some rain will fall and do its thing and never again find itself suspended in the clouds.

Where did it go?

Into our dreams, to make them all the more real. Into our lives, so we may move more quickly along. And, darkly, into our hearts, where it flooded.

The metronomic thump of the wipers was something I began trusting the years to. Beginning with yesterday, each thump became a moment, and falling back in time, these memories (all of them) strung out and formed a cord that threatened to fail. When I had reached a point far enough from my old home, I knew it would snap.

I chose for my course not the highways, but those sub-roads (tributaries) which few can say they've ever traveled. A leaf. Driftwood in undulation.

I drove until the light began to grey, turning everything to shadow. I found a Travelodge and paid with Visa and waited an eternity for the woman behind the counter to find me a pass key. She was elderly, silvery hair. Did she say her name was Josi? No, Josephine. Josi, she explained, made her sound cheap. I nodded—though I happened to like the name Josi—and retired to my room as quickly as possible without appearing rude.

Room Three.

I checked the bathroom, relieved myself, then unwrapped one of the tiny courtesy soaps and scrubbed my face clean. In the mirror I did not appear any older, only worn.

Leaving the bathroom, I surrendered the room to darkness and dropped onto an unusually soft bed.

"My brother, Arny, he used to call me José, you know, instead of Josi, like the Spanish name?" the woman's words still echoed in my mind from our earlier conversation.

The drapes on the window wouldn't close all the way and from the parking lot, ghostly light from mercury vapor lamps fell harshly onto my pillow, my face. I held my eyes open as long I could, wanting them to water. Hoping that if they did I might be able to cry. Hoping that once the pain set in again, the tears would put me under, an anesthetic, and I wouldn't have to bother with thought.

Thinking:

Only four days ago...

Pete had called. The clock in my study read 10:10 as I'd just stepped out of the shower. I usually slept until nine on weekdays, then wrote until Jeni arrived home from school.

"I'm really sorry Michael," was the first thing he said and I felt the Earth beneath me splinter. I thought: Moira? Jeni? Where were they? Moira: at the hospital. Jeni: school. But... no. That wasn't true. Jeni had a dentist appointment, and Moira was taking a few hours off work to drive her there.

I forced my eyes to remain open, but the lamplight would not oblige. Not now. I blinked. Not ever. Dry. Blinked again.

Nothing.

The covers were cool. I put one finger in my mouth. Sucked on it, took it out. Carefully, I put the wet finger to my right eye—so that it might get the hint—but my finger soon dried and I was alone on the archipelago, surrounded by the torrent just outside the motel walls.

Maybe if I just got out of bed? Yeah, hop into the shower... sure, that'd start the old eyes up. Better yet, take a stroll outside for a while...

"Now I lay me down to sleep. I pray the Lord my soul to keep. If I should—" and Jeni stopped, one night not so many weeks ago, kneeling beside her bed.

"What's wrong?" I asked.

She looked up at me. I stood there in the doorway.

"I don't like the rest of it," she said softly. The way she spoke, the way her lips moved, her eyes, reminded me of my mother. The way she would just take a step back and see an every-day *something* differently.

"That's alright, Sweetie," I told her, "You don't have to say any more if you don't want to," and was immediately rewarded with a smile. I stepped into her room again, scooped her into my arms and landed her in bed. Sitting side-saddle at the edge of the mattress, I gave as big a hug as I received.

"I'm really sorry I'm the one who has to tell you this," Pete droned on. Damn it, why couldn't he just shut the hell up?

Outside the motel, I listened as a car pulled up near mine. A succession of car doors opened and then closed. A family rushed beneath the narrow awning that hugged the building's facade. I listened to their feet smack the slick, puddle-pocked macadam. A young girl and boy complained about a stuffed animal that had fallen out of the car and gotten wet. The father led them quickly away to the office up front, where they most surely would meet up with Josi/José/Josephine.

Since I'd met Pete in college, I could never really pin him down. He was often vague and distant when it came to specifics—he never truly gave you a straight answer, one you wouldn't have to ask for further clarification on. I accepted this, however. No problem. We all have our hang-ups, some stranger than others. Pete always seemed to care in his own unique way, though. I began to think that I could go back to that afternoon (when he called with the news) and decide that this was the moment he changed. He seemed at the same time excited, tense and relieved. As I've said, he wasn't an easy person to figure out, and such a slight deviation in character was akin to catching shadows at midnight. And midnight was as good a place to begin as any; I'd already arrived.

And the rain. Would it ever end? I stared through the partition in the curtains and allowed the reflection of water to reflect a second time in my eyes, still wondering why I couldn't cry.

Did sleep ever come? I'm not certain. It's possible I lay there all night, imagining my unforgiving dreams fully conscious; it wouldn't surprise me to discover that I only thought I'd fallen asleep.

six

The following morning offered sun and I decided (against Pete's advice that I take my time and see the countryside) to drive the remainder of the way straight through. Twice I needed a restroom, first in Emporia and later just before Fayetteville, and my throat ran scratchy, begging for an icy Coke, but I persisted. I never gave much thought as to what my new house would look like—didn't really care. Now I was almost obsessed with it. I needed to know everything about it. Pete had said it was comfortable, the nondescript answer I'd expect from him. But how big was it? How extensive the property? Who lived there before me, or was it new?

I hated the time, the hours. Wanted it all to go away. I knew this was impossible, but I tried to keep it at arms length. Turn my back on it.

And this road, connecting the past and future. I couldn't help but think that even though I could turn back, the worn tarmac beneath me would never allow such a thing.

● ● ●

Where it should have been, it was not; I couldn't find the sign for the Sweetwater exit. All the other towns on the map were there, but not Sweetwater. Finally, after wasting another hour getting on and off the Interstate, I drove into a town named Middlehope, pulling into a gas station that doubled as a restaurant: Tiny Peco's. Inside were two men, one apparently a policeman, the other probably a local. I nodded hello. They did not. Taking my seat at one of the swivel-stools up front, I waited. There was no one behind the counter, no clanking of pots or utensils beyond. I took two blue packets of sugar from a plastic dispenser and tapped them rhythmically on the Formica countertop.

"Peek ain' here," one of the men said. I turned to face them; it appeared as if neither had spoken.

"Wife's sick," the scruffy cop intoned. The strongest gale could not muss his tangled crop of hair. I didn't quite feel like asking why *they* were there. Perhaps watching the store for Mr. Peco? I did, however, ask if I could get a glass of water.

"Doan want that," the cop drawled. I asked why. The other man's face broke out into a smile half-filled with dark, yellowed teeth. I felt suddenly stupid. And sick to my stomach.

"Wells are dry," he said, matter-of-factly.

"All of them?" I asked, unbelieving.

The cop didn't seem to care what I thought and slid a toothpick in between his lips, "Think what you want."

I stood up to leave.

"You're not from here, are you?" the guy with the

teeth (or lack thereof) asked. His voice was lackluster, each word falling to the oily tile floor beneath him like damp sawdust.

I told him no, then asked quickly if either knew where the town of Sweetwater was.

"Ain' no town named Sweetwater 'round here."

I nodded and made my way for the door, then stopped when he added quickly, "Sweetwater's 'bout twenty miles south'a here. Get back on the main road, take a left and keep goin' till you hit Mercury Street. Follow Mercury and there you have it."

"I thought you said there *wasn't* any Sweetwater."

"No town named Sweetwater, anyways. Community."

"It's a community? What kind of community?"

The cop stepped in with, "You sure are askin' a lot of questions."

The overall atmosphere of the place had grown unbearable. A sick, burnt-grease slickness clung to everything. I needed fresh air.

"Thanks for your... help," were my final words. I didn't look back, not even after I'd gotten into the rental. I took the man's directions and stopped when a small, weathered sign shyly announced MERCURY STREET. Another two miles and the road forked. In the center of the fork (floating in a sea of choking kudzu) sat another sign as decrepit and run-down as the first. I had to squint and experiment with the letters for a while, for they were nearly illegible. I managed:

SWEETWATER

LA VISTA   *WEATHERSTONE*
BLACKBERRY   *PHASE TWO*

I turned the key again without thinking, the car was still running, and jumped when the engine grinded. Of all the names given on the list, Blackberry was the only one mentioned to me by Pete. I considered myself lucky to have gotten this far on so little information. I should have at least asked for a quick sketch of the area. Something. *Anything!* All I had received from Mr. Pete Fausta was a quick (unreadable) smile and the terse words, "You'll find it."

I pulled warily onto the left fork.

seven

The road forked once again: La Vista and Blackberry Way. Taking the left onto Blackberry Way, enduring a mile of pocks, fist-sized stones and sinkholes, the road dead-ended in a small cul-de-sac. There were two houses, each built with an eye toward the Folk Victorian style and both set apart (almost staring at each other) as punished siblings, forced to arrive at some impossible reconciliation. I noticed the vans at once, four of them lined end-to-end in the driveway of the house on the left. I parked in the circle and walked down a lengthy drive. At the bottom waited a man in overalls; as he pulled open the back doors of a van, he turned to meet my stare, then went directly back to his work without further comment.

"Hey there," I tried amiably. He did not acknowledge. Assuming that this was *my* house, I asked if I could help with something. I was standing beside him, trying to look inside the van. All I could discern was isolated light within the darkness;

the screen of a computer monitor, perhaps, and then the monotonous blink of red and blue, on and off, then the man's shoulder as it blocked my view.

I then passed from curiosity to irritation.

"Mr. Dorigan?" a voice with deep resonance asked from behind me. I turned to face a small, yet imposing man, strong in build with hazel eyes that reflected not the blue sky behind him, but January ice-storms. He had the height of a teenager, yet nothing about him was child-like. I thought of how he addressed me. Not that he called me Mr. Dorigan, but rather how it was said. I compared it to the voices of the men I'd met in *Tiny Peco's*.

"I'm Michael Dorigan," I said, somewhat softly.

The man forced a smile and offered his hand. I took it, though reluctantly. The sun glanced off the golden watch on his wrist, the flare causing me to look away, eyes watering.

"Benson Aldritch," he said, then smiled some more. "Weren't really expecting you for another day or so." And then I realized what had been bothering me... His accent was anything *but* Southern. He sounded like a native New Englander. It took a moment for me to center myself.

"Well, to tell you the truth, I wasn't really expecting any of *this*," I said, motioning toward the vans, trying my best to ignore the man in overalls behind me, "Is something wrong with the water?"

"Come again?" the stocky man asked, eyeing me cautiously.

"These men aren't plumbers?"

Benson Aldritch laughed. I made a conscious effort to study the logo on the back of one of the workman's uniforms: three waves—one blue, one red and one gold. This same design was also emblazoned on the side of each of the vans, along with one word, WEATHERSTONE.

"Actually, Mr. Dorigan," and here he paused, "We're just running a final check on the house's security system."

"How long until you're through?" I asked.

"Hard to say," he said rather brusquely, all laughter forgotten, then pushed past me, entering the house through the open garage doors.

I took some steps back and for the first time really *saw* the house. It was nothing less than extravagant. The two-car garage could easily hold twice what it boasted. Inside, I watched Benson Aldritch pick up what appeared to be a cell phone; he dialed furiously. When he glanced up and saw me staring, he retreated further into the house.

Walking around to the back, I found an enormous split-level deck. Bay windows. The back yard was a great hill, sloping for quite a distance before leveling off into a dense expanse of forest, running forever into distant realms. The view was spectacular.

Moira would have—

Would have what?

Nothing. Nothing, leave me alone.

"Mr. Dorigan?" Aldritch intoned from somewhere behind me. I didn't turn around. Just stared down the hill that was my backyard. I could sense the other man standing close to the house. I didn't answer.

Footsteps on wet grass. Louder:

"Mr. Dorigan, we're going to have to ask you to leave for a while."

"Leave? But this is *my*—" and here I had to turn and face him.

"Just a few last things we need to take care of."

"Right," I said, and walked back around to the front.

I stopped when reaching a point halfway between my house and its sister, hearing something that chilled me. Music, playing on some distant radio, drawing me closer. I moved steadily toward the other house and was quickly upon it. Although both were nearly identical in construction, this one seemed somehow older... as if each had been built by the same crew on the same day, though through some strange aberration *this* one had aged a century. I fell into a daze as the music continued to pull me; sirens to my soul. And all I could picture was Moira, sitting across from me at *The Barnsider*, a favorite restaurant of ours back in Monroe, New York. Music filled the background there too, and the song was the same, "Take it Easy" by The Eagles. As I moved toward the open front door of the neighboring house, I sat before my wife in another time, swimming in the soft candle-glow that held us apart from reality. The waitress brought our drinks—rum and Coke for me, straight Coke for her. We weren't very hungry and decided to share a seafood platter.

I stepped up to the door (humming along with the music) and passed over the threshold. The interior was not as I expected. Where there should have been finely aged furniture, exquisite decoration and subtle ambience there was instead an atmosphere of unrestrained insanity. Completing the length of the hallway, I entered the living room.

All shades were drawn and the screens of at least eight computer monitors cast the walls alight in phosphoric green and orange. Reams of print-out rose from the floor like wild mushrooms, without pattern, without reason. All so frantic. In one corner sat a desk with a strange box on it. Leads from all computers entered it from the front, and a larger cable exited the box, snaking across the floor to a far window. Moving toward this window, I raised the shade and peered out onto the same slope of hill shared by my house. About twenty feet down the slope sat a collection of small radar dishes; instead of pointing upward toward the heavens, they were all arrayed to seek their information downward in the woods and hills beyond.

With music still redolent around me (pouring, it seemed from the walls and ceiling) I drank the notes and, like a potion, the living room was transformed and the walls fell away and again I found myself staring into Moira's eyes. We were young then (she twenty, I twenty-one) and had everything before us. She was already on her way to her nursing degree and I, well... I took those courses in college they said I needed to take. And I wrote; wrote so much that my grades began to suffer. I was passing, though, and what were grades to a young idealist? My parent's weren't too enthused about this attitude, but I somehow made it work. That year I saw my first short-story in print, receiving five contributor's copies and a check for fifty dollars. We'd been seeing each other for almost two years then.

Now I can't tell you that what she and I had was perfect, but I *can* say that what we'd found far surpassed any previous relationship. We had our share of problems in the beginning and it was I who nearly caused us to go our separate ways. I trusted her, that wasn't the problem. She told me she trusted me, but inside that trust I had the hardest time believing her. I needed to know that she loved me, needed it so bad that I nearly drove her crazy. I drove myself half insane, but after a while was finally able to tell her how I felt. It took some time, but she taught me a great many things. She taught me to trust her, but also to trust in myself.

The waitress brought our dinner and I picked at lemony, breaded shrimp. Moira toyed with one of the scallops, but never followed through. We sat and watched one another, sipping from our drinks. It was a week and a half before Christmas. The only time I can remember being even slightly nervous around her was then. When we met for the first time, there wasn't a single butterfly. I didn't really know it was coming. I hadn't a clue that I would be saying it. Maybe that's why it seemed like the right time.

"Let's do something different," I said.

She smiled, tiny dimples forming at the ends of her lips. I recalled some words from Peter Pan, of Mrs. Darling's one elusive kiss no one could quite get to. It waited there now before me. "What do you have in mind?" she asked.

"Well... we could go ice-skating."

She glanced out the window, at the flurry of wet snow that had plagued the day and continued into evening. I was smiling now, too.

"By the time we get our skates and dressed it'll be too dark out." Her smile was honed by a certain light in her eyes, reflecting the candle flame on the small, wooden table between us.

"I don't know then…" My brow furrowed in mock concentration and I searched the ceiling for an answer. When I found none, I said gently, "We could get married?"

The moment held on forever; we looked at one another not only in tenderness, but with a strong and driving conviction that we would never let anything happen to destroy what we had worked so hard to build.

She rose from her chair, and I from mine and we held each other tight. A few people were staring, but we didn't care. We weren't in a restaurant. We were somewhere else; a place made only for us. And we stood there in each other's arms, dancing slowly to piped-in music, the warm scent of perfume on her neck and she whispered ever-so-softly, "I'll never stop loving you."

"Would you like a root beer?" a voice asked from behind me. I turned from the window and *The Barnsider* and bliss. On the other side of the living room stood a scholarly man dressed down in jeans and sweatshirt. The thin, tortoise-shell glasses he wore caught some of the computer light and caused me to squint.

He managed a friendly enough grin that I immediately accepted as genuine. He stepped toward me with his hand held out. I took it with much greater passion than that of Mr. Aldritch.

"Marshall," he said tersely, then, more sincerely: "Marsh."

"Michael Dorigan."

"I know," he bowed his head almost shyly. "Are you moving in today?"

I told him I planned to, as soon as they finished

whatever it was they were doing.

"They still over there?" he asked as he looked behind me, eyes narrowing as if he could see through the walls.

I nodded, smiling, "Strange bunch of guys."

After a short silence, Marsh told me he'd just finished reading my latest novel the other day. Would I sign it for him? I told him it would be my pleasure, then: "What *is* all this…" I looked over at the computers, printers and stacks of paper, "If you don't mind my asking."

His eyes darkened before he spoke, his words sounding as if read from a teleprompter:

"I'm working on a survey of the area. With the dishes I can bounce waves back and forth and... We're looking for evidence of—" he stopped, hanging his head once again.

"Evidence of what?" I asked.

"Evidence of... a better land description for when we decide to expand."

"*We* who?"

"Weatherstone."

"Weatherstone," I repeated, more to myself.

"Root beer?" He pronounced it *rut*beer.

I pushed a strange confusion away, sighed then nodded, "Sure, why not?"

Marsh disappeared momentarily.

From outside, I listened as the fleet of vans began pulling out of the cul-de-sac. Moving quickly to the still-open front door, I watched them leave, a faint cloud of orange dust hovering inches over the ground in their wake.

Marsh had crept up silently behind me. I started when he touched a cold can to my bare arm, then gratefully accepted it. Together, we watched the departing vans shrink down Blackberry Way. The music was gone now. Perhaps Marsh had turned the radio off. Unless, after all, the melody had simply traveled forward through the years, through time, mysteriously guiding me on. This thought (though I recognized it as my impossible imagination) comforted me. Such awful comfort.

"Weatherstone," I whispered, merely repeating the word, lost in a dream of dancing in small circles in a far-away restaurant in a lost world.

The other man nodded, snapping open the tab of his own A&W.

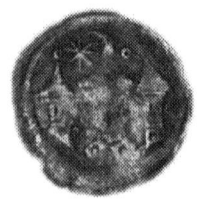

eight

My new house had absolutely no feeling at all. No life of its own. It sat stark and empty, save the rich smell of new carpeting. Walls without tack-holes or yellowing cellophane or crayon graffiti. I toured the house slowly, noting every nuance, putting it all to memory. The thing was, I felt as if I knew what waited around each corner. An exploding chain of déjà vu haunted my every step.

At the top of the only flight of stairs leading up, I turned to my right and continued down a hallway. At the end sat two doors. Both were open: a bathroom and a bedroom.

Jeni's bedroom! a voice inside insisted and I told it to shut the hell up, but it wouldn't listen and said over and over *Jeni's bedroom!, Jeni's bedroom!* until I finally turned away. Walking down to the opposite end of the hall, a small door sat ajar to my left. *Linen closet*, the voice said, and I imagined a tapestry of some homespun art (more déjà vu) just beside it. I somehow knew what this place would look like furnished. Lived-in. Actualized.

A set of double doors waited at the extreme end and I hovered slowly to a stop at this new doorway. I closed my eyes and for the first time forced away any thoughts of Moira or Jeni. Not because I didn't want them with me, nor because I wanted to forget... I just felt myself slipping again. Felt my grip on reality a fragile, tenuous one.

Opening my eyes, I found an empty hall. The doors were simply doors. I moved forward and entered the room, like walking into a converted cave, dressed and disguised to deceive.

My eyes swept the room and another uncertain, unwelcome current of precognition washed over me. I walked further in end and knelt to the floor, leaned close, studying the waxed planks of wood. It was the only uncarpeted room, beside the kitchen, that I'd come across. I leaned closer. The wood smelled fresh, but...

And then it clicked. There was dust. Not a lot—just a trace film, which is why it was so difficult at first to make out. With my finger, I traced a slow, meandering line before me. How long did it take dust to accumulate?

Depends, Mr. Mike, on how long you wait. On how patient you are.

I finally let myself down and stretched out, lying on my back. I examined the ceiling. A wood-slat fan and light looked down upon me. Still. Unmoving. I glanced across the room and noted the dimmer-switch that most surely would send its current through to the apparatus above.

I began to hum a song.

Then I looked at the floor again. Something peculiar. Spaced at intervals suggesting a large rectangle were four circular areas completely void of dust. The circles were about the diameter of my closed fist and I measured each to confirm this.

I don't know how long I remained there on the floor,

but when I shook myself awake, long shadows stretched out across the wood, dissecting the room, cutting my body into jagged, random sections. As I pushed up, my back and shoulders protested in angry masses of knots. The sun bled through a western facing window.

As I left the master bedroom and moved back down the hallway (toward the stairs) I wondered idly why there wasn't any furniture. If Pete had gone through so much trouble to set me up here, why forget a couch or a bed? Perhaps tomorrow it would arrive. After all, he *did* want me to take my time getting here.

In the kitchen, the sun bathed everything in a thick, syrupy red-orange. I noticed a simple folding table leaning against some bricks on the back patio. I pulled this table into the kitchen, in front of a set of bay windows that overlooked the hills and woods. There were also two paint-spattered stools as well. I set them around the table.

Who are you expecting for dinner, Mr. Mike?

Shut up.

A quick search and I found the cabinets bare, as well as the refrigerator, which hadn't even been plugged in. Not a stale Wheat Thin to be found.

I glanced at my wristwatch: 7:35. The sun reflected off of the small, round token of glass and cast an oblate sphere of light on the ceiling and walls. I toyed with this for a while, seeing what I could touch with this shaky light. Then the doorbell rang.

Pete?

No. He said he might drop by, but this wouldn't be for a few days. He was still back in New York, where I once had been. Or was it all a crazy fantasy? Orange County, New York? Monroe, Chester, Middletown, Sugar Loaf: all figments of my desperate yearning.

The doorbell again.

Benson Aldritch? Possibly...

I rose to meet the caller and was pleased to discover

Marsh's friendly countenance filling the open doorway. In one hand he clutched a sweating six-pack of A&W, in the other a family-size bag of sour-cream and onion potato chips.

I couldn't help but smile. Despite the strangeness of our meeting earlier, I considered myself lucky to have someone to talk with.

We sat at the table in the kitchen, watching the final tendrils of solar flare lick the tree-carpeted horizon. Marsh cracked open another can, handed it to me, then helped himself to one.

"You really like root beer, huh?" I asked.

The man grinned; plenty of fine, white teeth. A boy being praised. He was twice my age, yet seemed so innocent. I was still curious for a more in-depth reason as to what was going on in his living room, but right then all I cared about was his company. Grateful for it. Marsh said not a word. Sitting there in mutual silence, we stared into the west as the sky went from red to blue to deepest violet, burning coldly. Tiny stitches of diamond thread began to embroider the canvas of night. I could almost feel their solar breeze so many incalculable light years away.

The can of root beer remained cold in my hand.

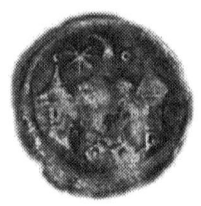

nine

When I dream, for the most part, there's usually *some* element of reality tucked inside the vision. Something I can look back on and say, "Now, wait a minute! So *that's* what made me have that nightmare!" This time it was so completely different.

I found a small fold-out cot in the linen closet upstairs and set myself up as best I could in a room adjacent to the den. No blankets or pillows. Still in my clothes, I fell asleep *instantly...*

...walking down the upstairs hallway in a dark, blue robe/toward the closed doors of the master bedroom/towel in my hands, drying my hair, listening to the television drone somewhere downstairs/the smell of fresh coffee/barefoot, soft steps on the carpet/I reached out to the doors to push them open *and...*

...sat up on the cot with two nearly forgotten words on my breath. My heart raced.

The words were, "Love me," which I whispered again into the morning, sweat pooling and stinging my eyes.

Still shaking off the sleep that clung like dull and tasteless syrup, I left the room and made it to the bottom of the stairs. Taking the steps two at a time, I reached the top and stood there in the middle of the hall. I turned to face the master bedroom doors; they were closed. As in the dream, I took one step forward, held my breath, forced back the vertigo, stomach spinning, don't pass out, don't pass out, *don't!*

I reached out to push the doors open.

There's nothing in there. I told myself this over and again, but some detached part of me thought quite adamantly that this was a lie.

A car horn bleated from somewhere outside. I stopped and let my arm fall to my side.

"Nothing there," I told the hallway, and the doors, then turned back to the stairs. The air felt strange. In the dream, it had been filled with a warm, familiar welcoming—now it was as if I were walking through an endless vacuum.

Once more, the complaining horn. Feeling sticky, my hair matted from sleep (mouth pasty) I walked down to the front door. Then, instead of the horn, there was the doorbell.

I answered.

Before me stood two pimply-faced gentleman in their early twenties. The way they carried themselves, however, belied their years. Cocky. Self-important. Symptoms of adolescence. "Mr. Dorigan?" one asked. It was difficult to tell them apart. I nodded.

"Is it okay if we get started?"

It took me a moment to realize that they had just arrived with the things I'd packed (*Pete* had packed) from the old house. I told them to go ahead. I was still trying to distinguish between the two. Brothers?

"Give me a few minutes and I'll give you a hand," I said.

Nodding, they walked back to the U-Haul.

After a quick shower, I directed them to start moving everything into the living room. I didn't have much anyway, didn't want our old bed or any of the furniture—what would I possibly do with Jeni's toys? Pete would take care of those things, as he said he would. Didn't want Moira's pillow, her favorite perfume...

Am I a convincing liar? I wish I were better at it.

Abandoning my promise to help them, I walked past the truck and around the house to the back yard. I thought of Jeni and how much she loved sleigh-riding and what an amazing slope this hill would offer—except, of course, for the abrupt declaration of trees and kudzu that began as soon as the land leveled out. Besides, snow didn't make South Carolina as permanent a home in the winter as it did New York.

Then again, we wouldn't have been living here anyway. Sweetwater was a place of circumstance. Eventuality.

I looked across to Marsh's property and studied the dishes that, at that moment, hummed slowly to and fro. If I hadn't known he had so much equipment inside, I might have seen them merely as satellite dishes snatching distant lands and pay-cable channels from the stratosphere. But even then I would have wondered... why so many? And why were they all pointing downward?

I made my way cautiously down the hill. At the bottom, I glanced back up. Marsh's house was lost somewhere to the left, but my own loomed above me, monstrous and damning. It was a large house, for sure, but from where I stood it appeared surreal and enormous; I was reminded of sitting in the front row of a movie theater as a child, straining my neck back, watching the giant, warped figures tower before me. If I leaned back any further and the land decided to give out, the entire structure might come tumbling down the hill in a frenzy, crushing my body. For a brief moment, it seemed as if the house's anger was based solely on my own stupidity. Something was happening. Something huge. The problem was this: I was looking in the wrong direction, missing the entire thing. Dizzy, I turned away and began to walk along the median of scrub-grass and trees. To my surprise, fifty feet from where I began, I discovered a narrow path. The ground along it was impossible to see at times, but it was obvious someone had been down here often enough to create the walkway. Probably Marsh. For all I knew, this land was his, not mine. Not that it really mattered.

The trail wandered a while in no particular fashion. When it began to fork, which it did more often the further I went, I started leaving markers: branches twisted and snapped into what were supposed to resemble arrows, pointing me back the way I'd come. I was amazed at how dense the foliage was! I could see no more than ten feet in any direction—just the path before and behind me. To look above, even, was to see only a narrow blue ribbon where the open sky should have been.

Soon, an odd sense of claustrophobia began to take hold; the air was oppressive. I started to turn back when I heard something. Water running over stones. Ripples. A stream. Somewhere nearby. Why hadn't I heard it sooner?

And then I realized it *wasn't* that close. It only sounded so because the afternoon was so completely silent. Not a bird, nor breeze. Just the woods that grew deeper and darker, seducing with whispers of evening and cool winds. I took my steps softly, allowing the sound of the stream to fill the void. I studied the sound as it wrapped itself around me, urged me on and I said yes. Soon enough, the sound doubled in volume, then doubled again and the path dead-ended. I stood at the bank of a small river perhaps fifteen feet across. On the opposite bank, I could see the continuation of the path. I had no intention of crossing. The ribbon that was the sky appeared broader above the river, and my breath came easier, not as labored. I let myself down onto the mossy bank and stretched out.

The air back on the path was thick, muggy and

steaming. Here, by the river, it felt almost like autumn. I even found a few of the trees further downstream turning premature shades of burgundy and gold; the sky, too, seemed thinner, cooler, a paler blue.

I shook my head. The trees were only dying. Everything dies. Well, almost everything. Some things are left behind. To tell the tales. To weep. To wonder.

It was then that I felt the eyes. I could, of course, see no one in the green around me. And surely there could be no one. I would have heard even the stealthiest of footsteps. But still... powerful, unseen eyes.

Forget it. Just your imagination putting things where they aren't and can't and shouldn't be, that's all. And I leaned forward to watch my reflection, careful I didn't slip.

My eyes, blue, seemed the exact shade of the sky given as backdrop, but there were dark crescents below them. I tried to smile, but in doing so I appeared a stranger, more drawn, less than what a young man of twenty-six should appear to be.

My hair was still slightly damp from the shower and a few strands lingered on my forehead, one almost in my right eye. I ought to get a hair-cut. Then I thought: why? What did it matter?

Mouth slick and gummy, I reached down into the clear water with one cupped palm for a taste. At first I could not feel the water on my hand, then (pulling it out) I noticed that my fingers were nearly numb. Touching them to my cheek, I recoiled in how cold they were and at once began to rub my palms together, searching for warmth.

First nothing. Then tingling. Then pins and needles and minimal pain, as if I'd almost gone as far as frostbite. But from a small river? A stream in South Carolina? And in the middle of the summer!

I examined my fingers again and the ruddiness began to fade. Looking at my reflection in the moving water, I peered past my distorted face into the current caressing the stone and clay bed below. I'd heard of water being unnaturally hot from factory runoff, but never cold. And cold to such an extreme. How was it possible?

I stood. Upstream, the water disappeared around a sharp corner. I thought briefly of following the river, perhaps gaining some clue as to its nature, but an overwhelming feeling of dread filled me the same moment the idea entered my mind. An unseen force of urgency nearly pushed me to the ground. I had to get out. The *eyes*! Watching me. This time I couldn't dismiss it as paranoia and I ran quickly through the cloying heat and steamy leaves, nearly missing the arrows I'd planted. When I finally emerged from the woods and looked up again to the monolithic specter of the house (still threatening to tumble down and destroy me) I collapsed to the ground and waited until I could again breathe regularly. It took some time, which was fine with me, since time was all I really had.

When my chest stopped burning, my heart stopped racing and my imagination ceased its soaring, I realized something. In all the past half hour or so of confusion, I hadn't thought once about Moira or Jeni. I had grown so accustomed to having their memories with me; it shocked me that they left for even a handful of seconds.

Had they truly left me, or was it I who was letting them go? I couldn't decide—feeling a painful tightening in my chest at the thought that they would not always be there to comfort me, even if it *was* for just a brief look back. The tightening grew heavier and panic flooded through me: I was having a heart-attack! But it soon passed. Only anxiety.

I lie there in emptiness, aching in the knowledge of their complete and total absence. The past would not help me now, only hurt—digging deep into my heart, mocking with familiar smiles and words and hugs from my wife and daughter who were no more.

ten

Sitting in the corner of the empty master bedroom.

I'd taken another hot shower, but still could not do away with the icy chill the river left with me. Left *in* me. The U-Haul twins were gone. I was alone.

I watched through half-closed eyes the shade and shadow. Sunbeams fell through the blinds, painting the floor in soft, buttery stripes. They were warm. They made me tired. I thought again of the dream I'd had earlier, of walking down the hall toward this room, but it seemed to fall apart the more I concentrated. Soon, I could remember only that there was a dream and no more. Mind swimming, I hovered in this state for what had to have been most of the afternoon. I think I heard someone at the front door a few times, though can't be completely sure. And though I tried not to think of anything but the soothing, yellow bars on the wood, I found myself recalling my last semester in college—my first *real* meeting with Pete. I could smell the cool, tangy scent of pine. Then, hidden beneath it, the slightest touch of airborne chalk-dust.

I was on the fourth and top-most floor of Tyner Hall, just outside room 402-A, waiting patiently for Dr. Fitzgerald. It was a Friday afternoon and I'd been standing around for almost an hour. The lights in the building had been extinguished; I passed a janitor on my way in who had just finished buffing one of the first floor wings. He nodded and I smiled. That was all.

I looked at my watch and found it nearing (rather slowly) 5:30 pm. From the other end of the hallway—just after the entrance to the stairwell—late afternoon sun made its way through a circular, stained-glass window crossed several times with thin, steel bars. The effect was confining... unnerving. Images filled my mind of institutions tucked safely away in the shadowy recesses of New England towns.

"Dorigan?" a voice behind me asked and I jumped, nearly shouted, then caught myself and found a familiar face. Not Dr. Fitzgerald, as I had expected, but a student I remembered from a previous class last winter. Odd that he knew my name after such a long time. Sensing my hesitancy, he offered his hand with the words, "Sorry I scared you. Peter Fausta."

And then I remembered the class we were in: Cognitive Psychology. The professor had memorized only our last names and apparently received great satisfaction in screaming them aloud whenever he desired our attention. I remember, most clearly, the only name he failed to shout correctly every single time: Pete's. Instead of Fausta, the old man would bellow, "Faustus!", and from then on we referred to Pete, much to his chagrin, as Dr. Faustus. And right then, in the darkening prison of the hallway—remembering the sad pun—I said, "Hey, Doc,"

And it was his turn to smile, possibly impressed that I had remembered.

I asked what he was doing sneaking around here on a

Friday afternoon, but he pushed the question aside with, "Who are you waiting for, Dorigan?"

I told him and he somehow succeeded in persuading me to follow him across campus—I hadn't intended on staying much longer anyway. The test I needed to make up would have to wait until Monday.

The sun was several thousand shades brighter outside and I had to squint to keep my eyes from watering. The flaming sphere would soon disappear behind the library at the far side of the quad, but right then it shed its fury full-force.

I kept asking where we were going, but he answered with miscellaneous trivia to change the course of questioning. And we walked. Or, rather, I followed. Down the quad, past the library, through a copse of trees we all had at least once sat beneath to study in relative peace. His pace slowed a bit as the sun broke through the ceiling of leaves above, warm and tumbling sequins in a sea of cooler breezes. I waited for him to say something, but he was silent and soon enough we moved again with purpose, continuing up a hill; the trees, mostly pines now, patiently allowed us passage. We emerged again in sunlight at the observatory.

It wasn't a large observatory by any means, a modest telescope housed within cylindrical walls, topped by an aluminum dome perhaps 25 feet in diameter. The astronomy classes used it and on clear nights they would set up smaller telescopes for the students to come by and peer through. Pete leaned against the small structure and looked to the western sky. The daylight was deep, ashen and did strange things to the color of his eyes. He motioned me forward and I sat with my back against the observatory wall. The sun found only those strands of hair the wind accepted—the rest of me was under its line of fire.

"Look," he said, standing before me. And I did: clouds scudded thoughtfully eastward. The Stillwater River moved effortlessly past us, sliding over stones and shadowy sediment.

"So many people," he began, the first of several

sermons on the human condition I would eventually come to endure, "So many try to reach for the stars, don't you agree?" I shrugged. Nodded. Sure, why not?

"They think all they have to do is defeat the sky, conquer the speed of light and all the answers will come knocking on their doors. Answers to questions they haven't even thought of asking. All fools."

And all this from a college junior who worked odd hours at a Laundromat across town. He sounded like some aged philosopher. And he believed every word he spoke. Nothing was for vanity. He would have driven me crazy, too, if he were always this way. He wasn't. He had his spells of grandeur for sure, but he was still "normal" enough to be around. I never saw him with anyone else. No groups from class. I'm sure he never had a girlfriend, which was why I found it strange (thinking back on this) that he decided to take me aside that afternoon.

He soon sat down beside me and continued with, "Do you know where the answers are, Dorigan?"

I shook my head. I would let no one else call me by my last name without holding some sort of grudge. With Pete, it somehow felt appropriate. Natural.

"The answers," he explained, "Are right here..." and he gently tapped the top of my head with his index finger. "Instead of reaching out, we should reach within. It's just that simple, why so many people overlook it, or disbelieve it. But in being so simple, there remains the extraordinary task of figuring out how to tap into this flood of knowledge. It's possible, though. I know it is. When our defenses are their lowest, when we're vulnerable... that's when the answers come through. Answers to the true meaning of why we're here. Why we act the way we do. How far we'll go. It's not until we've reached the point of collapse that the answers are made clear."

I suppose what impressed me most was how serious he was. Pete was no forgery. He obviously spent a great deal of time thinking, whether this was a good thing or not. We were a strange pair, but for some reason our seemingly opposite natures aligned: an intense philosopher/budding-psychologist and a directionless writer.

The sun went down, leaving us stranded in twilight to the hypnotizing sounds of the river and waterfall. We were proto-humans perched on the edge of a new Earth.

And the bedroom floor was dark, the window reflecting only select shades of the failing evening light. I could see fine in the dusk, though. Perfectly fine.

My stomach then decided to work, clicked on, complained. It had been some time since I had a decent meal— couldn't stop thinking about food; Moira's baked chicken.

Don't do it, Mr. Mike.

But I could almost *smell* it! The special way she made it with lemon and pepper, all floating before me as I sat there. I had enough. I stood and padded out of the empty room, numb and nearly starved. Collecting the keys from the kitchen counter, I locked up the house and took the long way out to the driveway, by way of the back door and porch. I wanted to see the back yard again and when I looked down the hill, to the trees waiting below, I could barely make out the entrance to the path. Nothing so terrible about it now. Nothing sinister. I listened for the freezing river beyond. Couldn't be *that* far out, could it? Scanning the tree-cover, I could discern nothing but dark and silent vegetation. I found it difficult to concentrate on any point for longer than a few seconds. Done with the search, I moved around the house toward the drive. Pete had reserved my rental car for two weeks (did he really expect me to be driving *that* long?) so I wasn't overly worried about getting the vehicle back in a hurry.

I'd worry later.

It was my appetite that drove me then; I was starving, though not entirely excited about stepping again into *Tiny Peco's*. At the same time, I didn't feel like driving any further than I had to. Tomorrow I'd go and do that grocery-shopping thing, but for now I needed only something to fill my belly.

Blackberry Way seemed twice as long my second time on it, as did Mercury Street. I could not read the small billboard announcing the streets in the rear-view mirror, but I guessed about where it should have been. So, negotiating backward the directions I'd taken getting to the house, I found my way to *Tiny Peco's* without much trouble.

The cop and the man I'd run into on my last visit were no where to be seen. For this I was glad. Peco, however, loomed behind the serving counter, glaring at me. I felt like turning around, telling my appetite, "Sorry, pal," but the man silently forbade such a thing. I moved across the room and found a seat at one of the middle stools at the main counter. A strange aroma hung in the air. The usual things first: charred burger and steak, ketchup, onion, grease, but then an undercurrent of something else. A stink. Like old sausage.

"Help you?" the huge man asked. He sported an apron several sizes too small which hung loose (untied) atop his belly. There were dark rings under his eyes, bordering on bruised purple, as if he'd been socked, and I supposed they were similar to the ones I had under my own. Then I remembered the cop, or was it the other man? They'd said something about his wife being sick.

I asked, cautiously, "How is your wife doing?" At once, his mountainous façade crumbled. His lips loosened from their tight stitch and his eyes watered. Wiping a lake of sweat from his cheek and then forehead with a shirt sleeve, he braced his bulky frame against the counter with both arms. "Still sick," he said.

I nodded.

"Doctor say she be okay in a while, but I heard him talkin'. Said there ain't much of a chance. My neighbor's wife, too. Eddie and Syl. She got the same thing."

"What's that?" I asked.

He shook his head methodically, "Bad water."

I recalled something I'd heard earlier in the restaurant

about the wells being dry.

A pause. He seemed to be looking off into space. Out the door perhaps, across the fields to his house, in through his bedroom window to the ghostly form of his dying wife.

I glanced around and paused. I noticed a small security camera tucked away in one of many dark corners. A sharp, red light blinked from above the dark lens. Something inside me rose and then dove and I felt as if I'd just fallen a great distance. Staring into its single, digital eye I felt naked.

Don't be stupid, it's just a security camera.

Security? In a dump like this? The most a would-be thief could hope for was ten in change from the register and the hardened grease on the walls. Hardly worth the effort.

Yet still in all this decay sat this camera; new, sterile, trying to hide unnoticed, a spider biding its time. I tried to look away. Couldn't. I was frightened by what it might try to see in me, though intrigued to discover who was on the other end.

My gaze was finally pulled away when Peco broke the spell with words:

"We're outta bottled water."

Smiling, I explained that I was just in for a quick burger.

He grunted, turned, pulled a patty from a small shoe-box refrigerator and slapped it on the grill. Thin streams of oily smoke rose as the meat first screamed, then howled, then softly complained as it cooked. He added a few rings of onion, a slice of green pepper (which began talking back to the burger) and just as everything reached a meaningful conversation, Peco again turned to me, eyes questioning:

"You here the other day?"

I nodded, "There were two men here at the time. One was a police officer."

"That'd be Den. Other's Phil. They're alright."

"And you're... Tiny Peco?"

The man smiled. "That was Mae's (my wife's) idea.

Called me Tiny since the day we met. Hell, I've never weighed under three-fifty since. Some joke, eh? Call me Peek, though."

I shook his hand and offered my name in exchange.

"Den say you're looking for Sweetwater. Find it okay?"

"Yeah. It's just kind of strange, though. All hidden and secretive."

"S'pose that's the way they like it," and he flipped my burger.

I asked who 'they' were. His answer wasn't a surprise.

"Weatherstone," Peek explained, "They came along two, three years ago. Said they'd change things. Bring people. Bring business. Wake this place up. Seems, though, like we're all fallin' asleep," and he smiled a bit.

I knew *I* felt like falling asleep.

He garnished my cooked burger with a thick pickle wedge and a sweating can of Coke. I thought of Marsh, wondered if he was sucking down another A&W.

"Married man?" Peek asked, claiming a diet cola for himself.

"I am," I told him.

Um, Mr. Mike...?

"Any kids?" he sipped from the multicolored can. I nodded, smiling, "Her name's Jeni."

C'mon, the voice inside was adamant. What do you think you're doing?

And then I lied and told him that Moira and Jeni were back in New York while I was here on business.

"Any pictures?"

And I reached for my wallet.

Why are you doing this?

Opened it.

The first picture was of the three of us, lounging on a blanket at the far side of Smith's Clove Park. First Annual Dorigan Picnic? Yes. As a matter of fact it was.

Close the wallet, Mike.

No.

The next picture was of Jeni. First grade.

"The bee's knees," Peek intoned.

I smiled. It wasn't as easy anymore.

Close the wallet now!

The smile faded.

The next picture: our wedding.

The air had suddenly pushed down, a dense tarpaulin; smothering. Sweat filled my eyes, stung. Dizziness. I closed them tight.

"You okay?"

I barely heard the words. Someone speaking through a pillow and white and red and black static filling my head. Darker. I feared I would soon pass out. World dimming...

"Mike?"

Two pillows now. Three.

"I need some air," I said, or hoped to have said, and stumbled as best I could across the vast expanse of restaurant floor that seemed never to end. I must have been walking slowly (it felt like moving against a strong current) for Peek was right there at the door. He set his hand on my shoulder. "You need a ride?"

I shook my head. Stepping out into the early evening, my head began slowly to clear.

"Want me to call your wife?"

As if struck with a brick, I turned and looked at the man as if he were insane, then realized it was me who was losing my mind. I was trapped, nowhere to flee, sanctuary a dream.

"How much for the burger?" I asked.

He told me not to worry about it. I pulled a twenty from my wallet, the smallest bill I had, placed it in his meaty hand and staggered toward the rental.

"Sure you feel up to drivin'?"

I didn't answer and felt bad. He was only trying to help. Jamming the key into the ignition, I set the car into motion and the rear wheels chewed and spit gravel.

The walls were closing in again and I needed an answer. Any answer.

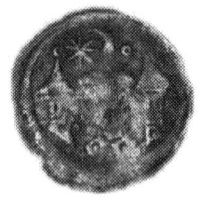

eleven

By the time I reached the house, I'd allowed denial to cauterize the wounds. I simply refused to think about the entire episode (why I had lied like that) and moved on. The outdoor lights were out, but I made it to the front door without injury, glancing over to Marsh's and making out only a soft glow from his living room windows.

After clicking on my front porch lights, I walked back toward the other house. The sky was overcast and all was grainy darkness; not 'evening' dark, but closed-closet dark. Everything still. On Marsh's porch, I rang the doorbell. Waited.

Nothing.

I knocked, and just as I took my hand away, the door swung inward. Marsh's face seemed a part of the darkness, hinted at harshly by the distant light from my porch. His countenance was automatonic and I found myself uneasy.

"How 'bout another root beer?" I asked, hoping to dispel the moment, break his trance. He opened the door wider and I stepped in, following him directly to the living room. He turned slowly toward me.

"Marsh, what is it?"

"I'll get you a cold one," he said flatly, then moved away before I could speak.

I walked among the glowing terminals and printers and stacks of read-out. The light from the screens caused the room to waver, shift, bend. I felt as if I were in some strange aquarium. I moved to one corner of the room, to a terminal flanked by an empty row of A&W cans, an empty cardboard tray that once contained a microwave dinner and several crumpled bags of sour-cream and onion potato chips. On the screen danced a continually changing array of numbers and symbols. I could make nothing of them, except for a single word at the bottom.

Flashing:

>>> *POSITIVE SCAN* <<<

Beside the keyboard I noticed about a dozen or so safety-sealed, foil packets containing shiny, translucent blue capsules. At my feet were the discarded remains of at least sixty or more of these packets. I scooped up all the capsules on the desk then spun quickly around.

Marsh stood there with an open can and stared me down maliciously.

"What are you doing?" he growled, advancing on me. It was so disconcerting seeing him like this. He was almost upon me, face livid; a vein thumped dark purple at his forehead. Then suddenly he slowed, stopped, his face loosening. He bowed his head and his voice changed dramatically. He sounded almost ashamed as he held his hand out, palm up.

"Can I have those, please?" he asked.

"What are they?"

"Medicine."

"For what?"

He paused, still looking down.

"For my headaches."

"Marsh, I'm not a doctor, but this isn't Tylenol. Where'd you get them? Who gave them to you?"

Rage began to well within me. I didn't know why— couldn't stop it. My emotions were a twisted thing, and I wasn't ready to go sorting through them just then. All I knew was that, for some reason, he was addicted to these things. It didn't make any sense. I was angry. I was emotionally and physically spent.

"Please," he said, groping for them. I held the packets behind me. It sickened me to see him like this. I'd only just met him, yet still felt some kind of bond. It was as if we were on the opposite ends of an unseen, but common link. Brothers of a sort. Whatever it was... I was so tired. Although I suppose I acted cruelly, I went ahead and used the pills as bait, questioning:

"What are all these computers for?"

His face pinched, "No... give me—!"

"If you want them, you'll tell me." He didn't move.

"Where did you get the drugs?" I asked.

"No..." he whined, softer.

"C'mon Marsh! I'm through playing around, now tell me where you got the damn capsules!"

Sinking to his knees, he breathed, "Weatherstone."

"What the hell is Weatherstone?"

Babbling, crying, "I don't want to go down there..."

"Where?"

"They drink lost souls... "

"Marsh, what are you—"

He collapsed, "Give them to me."

I held the foil packs out before him, "What are they for?"

"If I do my work, I get them every week."

"From Weatherstone?"

He nodded, trying to reach for them. I pulled away and he fell back to the floor.

"What does Weatherstone do?"

His eyes were red and swollen, "It's just a cover. Alternate energy resources lab for water. You're part of it. So am I. We all are."

Water?

I thought again of my talk with Peek. The wells: dry. The water: poisoned. But what reason could they possibly have for killing off the townspeople? Unless it was an accident... I figured I was beginning to draw false conclusions.

Then why had they gotten this man hooked on drugs? The moment I walked in he appeared on the verge of a mental breakdown. It was still in his eyes. Something familiar. And then I saw it: he was scared. Terrified!

I was nearing the breaking point again myself. I told him I would come back tomorrow morning. That we'd talk then. There was no point going on in the state we both were in.

He moved his head slightly, so slight I could not at first decide if it was a yes or a no. He appeared as beaten and whipped as I felt. I tossed the foil packets onto the pile of potato chip bags. He leapt at them.

"Tomorrow," I told him, a father scolding his son, and swam out of the tainted aquarium.

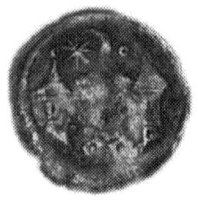

twelve

Still starving (I hadn't touched the burger at the restaurant), an overwhelming need to feel the softness of a bed beneath me— even if it *was* an old cot!—overrode all other channels. I moved determinedly across property lines and when I stepped onto my own driveway, something beneath my left foot rolled. I knelt and picked the object up and kept going, through the front door, stripping off my clothes as I moved through the rooms. Stopped. Finally, in the first floor bathroom, I placed the object I'd found on the bathroom sink and filled the basin. Dipping my hands into the near-scalding water, I brought it to my face, allowed it to flow into my skin, move to the rest of my body; forcing out the cold, demanding it out.

And it almost worked, too, but I had to open my eyes. Had to look down on the sink counter. There sat a familiar ball-point pen with the words *MCWHORTER FUNERAL HOME* embossed on its side.

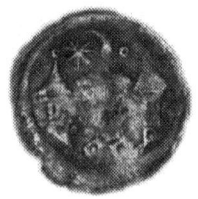

thirteen

In a dreamy haze, down the hall once again; the smell of fresh coffee. The blue robe I wore bunched comfortably at my shoulders, a terry robe. Quite warm. I moved slowly, floating it seemed, toward the closed double bedroom doors. And I began to notice certain things. The walls were painted a different color. Not white, but green. A deep forest green. On the wall to my right sat a framed picture, an oil painting of the ocean, a small bungalow set in swaying reeds and grass and just the hint of water past distant dunes. To the left hung a familiar Cherokee tapestry, though I could not remember having ever seen it before.

From downstairs drifted the non-intelligible, half-mumbling of a television. I dried my shower-damp hair. Words whispered at the borders of my mind. I stopped before the doors.

What were the words? I could almost hear them, could almost...

As I reached for the doorknob, a static rush filled me. I started awake.

The sleeping mind not only colors out of the lines, but does it so well you come to accept there *aren't* any lines—as we perceive the waking world. As I sat up, the final echoes of the dream burned away to nothingness. I could still feel the doorknob under my hand. My eyes were still closed, though, for I was trying to hold onto something else. A scent. Something sweet. Just beyond the door... soon it, too, was gone and I opened my eyes and the tiny guest bedroom waited stupidly around me. White, empty walls with nothing to say.

And then, with a growing permanence that took on several different forms of fear, I remembered the pen. I knew I'd have to go and see. I didn't want to. I *had* to.

And (damnit!) it was there the same as it had been last night, resting menacingly on the sink. I left it there again and walked into the kitchen. Five red and blue tumblers (which I had unpacked after the movers left) sat on the counter and I took one, turned on the faucet and filled the cup. Then:

What about the wells? This one certainly hadn't dried up. And what about the poisoned water? I'd already showered in it, certainly tasted some of it under the needle-fine spray.

I brought the tumbler closer and smelled the liquid within. Nothing unusual. Glancing at the kitchen table, I noticed a near-empty can of root beer. Certainly flat.

I did not believe my tap water was infected. I took the slightest sip. Then another. Then a swallow. Then waited.

No convulsions. No fever.

I drank what remained and headed upstairs for a shower—thinking back to painting our old bathroom back home. Moira and I had debated for weeks as to the color, finally settling on burgundy. We went to a paint store in Middletown to pick up the required cans only to discover there were over thirty shades of *burgundy* to choose from. We emerged from the store two hours later, four cans of "Autumn Fire" heavier.

After showering, I found myself yet again in the first floor bathroom, forcing myself to pick up the pen—to actually hold it. Was it possible that it was the very same I had signed the papers with so many miles north? I couldn't hold the thing any longer. I set it back down.

In the living room, I unpacked my typewriter and set myself up as best I could in what would be my new den. The best place I could find was a wide shelf next to a window. Soon, I'd go and purchase a desk or something. A comfortable chair. A bed. I just didn't feel up to it then. Didn't feel up to anything. I turned the machine on. Electric hum. I rolled in a sheet of heavy bond paper and stared at it.

Typed, **MOIRA**

Strangely, it didn't quite feel right. The keys weren't as stiff, they moved up and down with a fluidity I'd never experienced. Looking closer, it seemed as if the machine was young again. It shined. Not a scratch or speck of rust on the metal casing. Brand new.

I stared some more.

Stared for a long time.

Typed, **PETE**, then rose and found myself in the bathroom again, staring at the pen:

MCWHORTER FUNERAL HOME

If Pete had actually been here... but why? He would have told me he'd be taking a flight, wouldn't he? He would have said something!

I took the pen.

Clicked it on.

Off.

Put it in my pocket and walked outside.

The mid-afternoon heat was overwhelming at first. I've had my share of summer days before, but New York heat paled in contrast to Carolina heat. At Marsh's front door, I found a yellow scrap of note-paper taped at eye-level. "Gone for a walk." was all it said, and in the upper left corner was the same logo I'd seen on the fleet of vans the day before: three waves, and above them the word WEATHERSTONE. I took the paper, folded it in two and placed it in my wallet. I assumed the note was for me, given Marsh even remembered our conversation last night. I knocked on the door a few times anyway. Rang the bell. No answer.

With the opportunity presented, I walked around to the back of his house. The satellite dishes were smaller than I had at first thought. Standing behind them, I tried to judge exactly where they were currently pointed. Although all were stationary, a soft hum (not unlike my typewriter) issued from some hidden mechanism in their housing. On the back of the dish I found the same three waves. The same word.

The trajectory of the machines fell to some point a mile or so back between our houses. Walking, sliding at times on patches of pine-straw and clay, I managed to descend the hill and quickly found the entrance to the path I'd taken earlier. A few feet in, I stopped. Listened. The sounds of summer were in abundance. Birds. The wind in the ever-present fir trees. The soft and leathery whisper of magnolia leaves. Nothing like the dead monotone I'd experienced yesterday. I felt relaxed, peaceful.

With great care, keeping my gaze to the ground, I began to search for the branch-twisted arrows. There should have been one at the very first diversion, but the ground was clear. Remembering I'd taken a right, I went on to the next fork, but still could not find a marker. Perhaps some birds had taken them, or the wind...

Oh, right. That's great, Mr. Mike. Birds. The wind! Maybe a couple of flying monkeys just swooped on down and carried them off to Oz.

Had Marsh removed them? The good Mr. Aldritch? Tiny Peco's wife come sneaking off her death bed? Regardless of who it was, someone had removed them. That meant one thing for sure: someone knew I'd been down here. Someone knew I'd found my way to the freezing river.

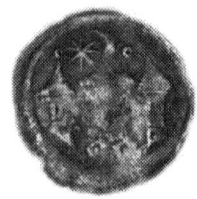

fourteen

Intermingled with the organic tang of wet leaves and earth was a deeper smell. Musty. Old. I continued down the paths, turning right and left with no thought as to how I'd later retrace them; Hansel minus one sister and a fistful of breadcrumbs. Didn't matter. I'd get back somehow. I had to go on.

In my right hand was the pen. I held onto it fiercely, squeezing it in my palm, wishing it would break. I'd been walking for nearly a half an hour when I noticed it again. I wished I was wrong, but the longer I waited, the clearer it became:

Silence.

I thought that I'd again reached the freezing river, but there was no water. Only silence. And that smell. Stronger now. Heavier. Thicker.

Without warning, the path dead-ended. Just like that.

Before me was the same thick stew of vegetation that pushed in from the left and right. And it was crazy, but just like yesterday afternoon I felt *eyes* upon me. Someone, something watching. Around me. Inside me.

Listening... but there was no one. I even considered calling out for Marsh, but held it back. For some reason the thought of breaking the silence scared me. I looked around. The sky was almost entirely obscured by the heavy limbs above. Verdant dusk. Then something in the flora caught my attention. A darker area within the green. Nearly black. I moved closer, put one foot into the woods, but kept the other firmly set on the path. I could now discern rock, huge and dark, but that was all. Growing bolder, I allowed the greenery to engulf me and pushed further in.

Camping with Moira and her parents a year after she and I met: Moira kept on assuring me that her Mom and Dad just loved me, but I was still nervous around them.

We'd gone up past Harriman State Park to an out-of-the-way site very few people frequented. By the time we finished clearing the ground of stones and acorns and had pitched camp, the sun had begun its descent. The Catskills were an unpolished emerald expanse across the horizon and in more than one place I noticed thin, spinning ribbons of chimney smoke rising from distant, unseen houses.

Our final order of business was the gathering of wood and kindling. We split up to hasten the task and in no time I found myself wandering aimlessly, timber in arms, with absolutely no idea where I was. Every now and then something would look familiar, but I could never be sure.

Just before I miraculously rediscovered our camp-site, the woods had thickened to the point where I could see no more than an arm's length before me. Choking in the leaves, the sun forever gone.

I was there again, though could have no hope of accidentally happening upon Moira and her parents. Would never discover the glowing embers of a campfire. Only the immense rock, growing larger. And something dark upon its side... another ten feet and I was there.

The darker area was revealed as a cave, though not precisely a cave. Nothing so natural. Rather a rock formation that seemed to offer an open doorway, hidden in the nightshade, with spiral limestone steps in descent. I looked up. Listened. Still nothing, except the eyes, bearing down, heavier than before. Demanding something I had no idea of how to give. I tried to ignore it, but the damn thing wouldn't stop. I had to get away.

But the house is so far...

No more than a three or four minute run...

But the trails. Remember *them*? 'Course you do! And this time you forgot the arrows.

No breadcrumbs

The eyes. Watching. Closer. Heavier. Impending.

Go down then.

No.

Why not?

Because.

Great excuse, Mr. Mike. You're an original.

I'm afraid.

Of what?

I don't know.

I was caught. It was just as difficult contemplating an escape down the stairs as it was making another run back to the house, hoping to lose the eyes. A run that would probably never end, for I had no idea which way to turn. Couldn't think straight.

Then how did you get here? How did you know which paths to take to get to this cave? You walked straight to it.

How?

I had no idea.

Just standing there drove me crazy, a paranoid torture that simply would not let up.

Then go in! Go down into it!

No.

Heavier. Closer.

Down.

Stop!

Down.

Damnit, please stop!

But I couldn't. Couldn't stop any of it. Completely beyond control. So heavy on my mind, and then my body; I felt physically restricted. Gravity now took on new dimensions, bending space and time toward a deeper well with every breath I took. I was compelled to go down. Anything to escape. And so I did. Kneeling, my body fit almost perfectly through the smooth stone. Perhaps I wouldn't feel so heavy further down... In my current state of mind, this thought took on all the merits of complete and unconditional truth and sanity. And the smell of earth and clay and dampness and moss and old things: an overwhelming deluge that filled the enclosed atmosphere entirely. At the same time it seemed to complement the moment perfectly, then exist in utter discordance. Not that I was trying to *look* for it—there was nothing but the cool pressure of stone at my sides and a gentle breeze from below which carried a lingering sweetness from the darkness.

Further.

Down.

And then a voice, though I couldn't make out the words.

I tried to concentrate on the slurred syllables, but they would grow no more coherent. I wanted to ignore it, but it was all I had next to the darkness and moisture.

Further.

Down.

When the passage opened, an eerie luminescence fell upon me. Where once I had to crouch and crawl, I could now stand upright. In the widening tunnel, I turned to the right and from around the corner a faint, purplish light clung tenuously to the walls.

The voice was louder, though still incomprehensible. I could more clearly discern, however, a pattern. Whatever the words were, they were being restated over and again, monotonously, maddeningly.

It was strange, but it felt as if all the answers were beyond this turn of stone. All I needed to do was to walk around and accept it. My mind was nearing a point where I could no longer retain even the slightest grip on sanity. My feet decided to betray me and would not move forward. I lost control, all frequencies jammed. I could do nothing but search for some way out. Not only out of this place, but my mind. Out of it all because it was simply impossible to see things for what they truly were anymore. The whispers I could not understand, louder, stronger. I realized just then how much I truly depended on my family. How much I, deep within, *needed* that support to build the rest upon. Nothing to hold it together now. No glue. Things floating inside me without purpose or meaning.

I took one step forward, mouth dry, and stared straight ahead as I forced yet another step forward. The light grew only the fraction of a shade brighter.

The mumbled words louder, though much more sibilant, harsh. I could almost name it.

More steps. Moving.

Quicker.

Rounding the corner, I stood before a room (though not really a room) of gigantic proportion.

The rushing of water (*Water! Must it always be water?*) flowing from a point of elevation nearby. Metered. And within this, two words—though they came entirely from my own mind and not the water:

Love me love me*lovemeloveme...*

Painful. Deep.

lovemelovemelove...

I watched as water spilled from a near-symmetrical gouge in a wall of stone to my left. Falling furiously, it filled a deep depression below. This pool, in turn, gave way to a stream, then a small river the width of the one I'd seen the other day. I felt completely dehydrated. Needed to drink. It seemed so clean! So clear! My throat cried a song of thankfulness as I knelt to the bank.

Would it numb my fingers as before? I tested cautiously with a finger and... no, it was not cold, but seductively cool and refreshing. With cupped hands, I scooped and brought some to my lips. Drank deep. I could not have been happier just then. I took more, swallowing, allowing it to fill me, calm me.

Sprouting around me were hundreds of tiny flowers. Moira knows a lot about flowers (you mean she *knew* a lot about flowers, right?) and I could at once name them: Asphodel. The sweetness I smelled before at the entrance were of this precious flower.

I continued to drink, the water now a part of me. I looked down into it and watched the bottom glimmer. But what was causing it to shine so? I looked up, trying to decide upon the light source. No over-heads. Nothing electric. Just a strange seeping that fell from in and between the root-ensnared ceiling. As my gaze fell, I noticed (for the first time) that an incalculable immenseness stretched out before me, far on the other side of the river. It was obscured, though, by an opalescent pall of fog and mist. I could see clearly no more than twenty feet from the opposite bank, but felt the limitless expanse.

I stood and tried not to step on the flowers; what were they called again? I couldn't remember. Their scent assaulted me, filled my head. Made me dizzy.

I knelt down for another sip, then stopped and looked again at the blossoms. Didn't I know their name just a minute ago? I couldn't be sure. But—

My mind shifted.

Everything shifted.

What were they called, damnit?

Then something else was missing, almost escaping notice. I had absolutely no idea where I was or how I'd arrived here. I noticed that my hands were wet, but could not recall dipping them into the water. I looked up. The sky was overrun with roots and rocks and—

Where *was* I?

I nearly screamed as I tried to recall my name and couldn't. The feeling left me hollow and scared... impossible to think in one direction, couldn't remember anything. I could only visualize an odd rapid-fire strobe of random bits that possibly were or were not my life.

A hand on my shoulder.

A man stood above me.

I tried to speak.

And night fell.

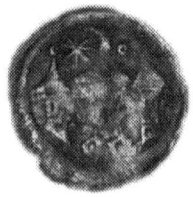

fifteen

The flicker of a candle, momentarily caught, then out. A breath of night. Then once again, the light, stronger, and the candle burns. I try to focus, try to define its center, but instead my vision blurs. The candle splits in two, then again and there are four. A new scent fills the air, with voices singing. My eyes are closed, and yet I see myself at a table with a woman and young girl. The birthday cake before the girl glows softly, illuminating her gentle face. I cannot tell where the song ends or begins. The candles are never blown out. The cake never eaten. Trapped in a slow-motion replay deviating in no set direction. A snapshot. And I know these two people!

Soon, the dream image begins to fade, though I try to hold on. The candles on the cake slowly reform. From four to two, then two to a single taper that swims in the darkness that is all I know. All I ever knew.

"Michael?"

I opened my eyes. The rim of a paper cup was pressed to my lips and I drank; the liquid soothed. The man hovering above me smiled. And then, as if thinking something over a second time, he frowned.

He offered me another swallow and I took it. But not of water, no. Of icy root beer.

Then a name came to me: Marshall.

"Marsh?" I asked.

He whispered, "Thank God," then moved away, out of the room. I tried to sit and nearly rolled off the bed I found myself in. Darkness melted slowly; a blue-green film coated the walls and seemed to waver like reflected light on an amusement park water ride. Marsh walked away and I waited for the dizziness to pass.

Convinced I'd regained enough strength to rise again, I stood shakily and found myself in a small room lit at the opposite end by a single, green-phosphor monitor. Why all this aged computer equipment, I wondered. All the hardware appeared to be at least ten or fifteen years old. Bargain basement stuff. *Museum stuff.*

Down a familiar hallway, I found Marsh sitting contemplatively in the living room. His eyes were serious, less frantic than that of last night. I moved a few stacks of read-out aside and sat down beside him.

And then I thought: my name is Michael Christopher Dorigan. Yes, and wasn't it wonderful? I felt whole again. I was me.

I looked up at Marsh. His hair seemed greyer, his face older as he watched me. I wanted to look away, couldn't hold his stare. Such a contrast from the other night when he'd acted no older than ten. Now I felt like a child who had done something wrong. When he spoke, it was with knowledge, though based in some foreign vein of reason. At first he cleared his throat, then adjusted an ancient pair of spectacles (ones I'd never seen him wear until then) at the end of his nose. "There's something going on," he said, then let it go for a while at just that. The look on his face was devastating, terrible, enigmatic. He began:

"I was teaching a special course in artificial intelligence a few years back at Cal Tech when a man approached me. He offered a substantial sum of money if I'd agree to work for him. For his company."

"Weatherstone," I whispered, the word falling naturally from my lips.

Marsh nodded. As I listened to him, I could actually hear that he had once been an instructor. He told me how strange it had been at first working in a laboratory, as opposed to the lecture hall, but he'd eventually grown to enjoy it. He'd even achieved a number of breakthroughs, ideas which Weatherstone compensated generously for.

"What I found strange," he continued, "were the people I worked with. Not that *they* were strange, but rather where they'd come from: nearly every last person had at one time worked at Cal Tech. Some were even students of mine. It was an entire year before I learned that a good friend of mine, Fitzgerald Brace, worked not three floors above my lab out in California..."

For a second, I stopped. Stopped breathing. Brace. I searched, dug, scavenged and eventually extracted the tiny nugget. Dr. Brace. My old statistics professor back at the University of Maine.

Marsh was talking, and I again tuned in: "...understand why. I still don't. Anyway," he leaned forward, "that was only the beginning."

The beginning of what? I wanted to ask, but my heart fell as I watched his eyes darken.

"I've been working here, in Sweetwater, for the past eight months. And as you've probably guessed, things aren't going well."

I glanced over at the computer on his right and saw three foil packets of the same small, blue capsules.

He followed my stare, explaining, "They put it in my

food first, without my knowledge. Then they stopped, and I started getting sick. *Real* sick. When I told them about it, they gave me an envelope and sent me on my way. In the envelope was a number. Twenty-two. A room number. Not knowing what else to do, I took an elevator, found the room and realized just how stupid I'd been."

He paused here. An awful pause. Too long. Too drawn out. I wanted to stand, but reasoned against it. It was better that I sat.

"It was something new," he explained, "The drug, I mean. They didn't give it a name, but made it clear that I couldn't get it anywhere else. If I wanted more, I'd do exactly what they said and…"

"And?"

"And didn't tell anyone what was going on."

It was my turn now, and after a breath I asked him to tell me what the hell was going on.

From the other end of the room a printer came to life.

The staccato rhythm filled the near-silence completely, a snare drum inside my ears.

Marsh made no motion to move, even when the printing had stopped. This new silence was worse. I rose to a crouch and walked on legs that were half-asleep to carefully tear the perforated sheets from the machine. Walking back to Marsh, who had slunk further down into his chair, I stood above him and saw the toll this had taken on him.

Then I looked down at the paper:

HELPMEDADDYHELPMEMICHAELHELPMEDADDY

I not only saw these words, but heard them as well. The voices echoed, filling my head, sounding so strange, through a tin can. I felt myself slipping again, wanting to sit down.

"What… is this?" I asked.

Marsh didn't look up.

"What is this!" I screamed, and he put his hands to his head, as if by doing so I'd magically disappear or something. No beans, Marsh. It's not that easy.

I found a firmer stance and kept my balance. "I want you to tell me about the woods. About the river. Tell me just what the hell you're doing here, addicted to some drug, sitting in a room filled with old, humming equipment." I paused, and before he could speak added, "And don't tell me you're surveying the land, either, because that's bullshit!"

He whispered something, but I missed it. I felt guilty. Whatever was going on was not entirely his fault—or any of it. I somehow knew this. Felt it. Marsh was as much a victim here as I was.

I leaned closer, set my hand on his shoulder. When he looked up, I asked him to repeat what he'd just said.

His mouth moved slowly, lips trembling, "There's something down there."

"What?" I asked, "In the woods?"

"Yes."

"What?"

"Something bad."

"C'mon, Marsh, just tell me what it—"

"I *can't* goddamnit!" he shouted, tears in his eyes, lower lip trembling. "When I found you before, I thought you were dead. But you weren't supposed to die."

Recalling the strange disorientation and fragments of what had happened, I said, "I thought I was dead, too."

Again, Marsh whispered, and I leaned in closer to hear, "We can't get out. We're trapped. There's nothing we can do. I can't tell you certain things, Michael, because they've done things to my mind. I don't really understand... but believe me, you can't ever leave."

I was so close to him, smelling the fear on his breath; couldn't move away.

"Why can't I leave, Marsh?" I asked with a burgeoning sense of lost hope.

He looked down at the floor, through it, past the polished floorboards, each word a deadening weight.

"You can't leave Hell," he breathed.

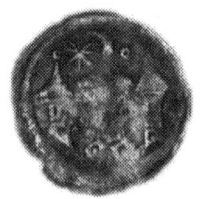

sixteen

I looked up at the sky, watching the purple deepen. It seemed whenever I *did* look up (for answers, for anything) it was night, or near night.

Marsh was unreachable. When I left him, he would no longer respond to me at all, crying, head in his hands, growing all the more upset and speaking of Hades and the Underworld. I figured he was still riding high on his pills. I tried my hardest to concentrate on the sky and watched the darkness bleed the life from it.

"Don't worry, it's comin' back," Jeni told me once when I had said I wished the day wouldn't end so soon. It was late spring and our first barbecue of the year. The grill glowed softly, each nugget of charcoal reduced to an insubstantial cinder cone. The wind had picked up and tousled the surrounding trees. I was looking forward to at least another half-hour of daylight to read by in the back yard. Jeni sat near the swing set, playing some game (*Candyland*, I think) with a few of the neighborhood children.

"Don't worry, it's comin' back."

I wasn't worried, standing there between the two houses, my gaze constantly shifting to the satellite dishes, though I wasn't so sure (this time) that it was ever coming back. The day was a tired thing, too exhausted to keep going. Light was a cover, an mid-autumn costume, a cruel trick. With darkness there is no physical sight, only a deeper awareness, and sleep.

From Marsh's living room window the heretical glow of his computers suddenly flickered, as a candle flame, then blinked out. There then should have been only the night, but something still held it back, postponing the final darkness. I looked back at my house and couldn't figure out why it was there. It shouldn't have been: from upstairs—hushed orange light diffused by curtains in the window of the master bedroom.

Had I left the light on?

When I first stepped out Marsh's front door, I pushed it all back, everything, all he said, all that had happened to me. The evening was real and I clung to it... then a shadow moved up in my window. A shape. No matter how much I tried to discount it, I could not pretend it away.

Then it came again, just behind the curtains.

Curtains? But there hadn't been any curtains in the window. The room was bare.

Remember the clear circles in the dust, Mr. Mike?

Yeah, but—

I began to force an answer from myself. Who was it? Couldn't be Marsh. Someone from Weatherstone was my first real guess. Aldritch?

I reached into my pocket, still staring at the orange-yellow stamp of light high above, and withdrew the pen from the funeral home. Clicked it on. Off.

Could it be Pete? What reason could he possibly have for being up there? The pen... I know, I know, the pen, but—

But what? Something's going on and there's a good chance Pete has something to do with it. Maybe even a *better* chance.

I looked into my driveway. It was empty, my car parked in the cul-de-sac. The shadow in the window came once more, then dissolved to the right. A confused moment of recognition and searching, then:

The light went out, and all floated. All was void. It felt so wrong. I couldn't move. Really couldn't. My body was a tightening vice, each segment (my legs, arms, head) slowly rendered useless. Darkness. Breathing it in. I felt both safe and completely exposed. Darkness. With Moira and Jeni, in their graves.

Stop it!

With them in their caskets... but it's a tight fit, no room to breathe, can't see!

Something kicked in, some mental switch, and I ran. Ran blindly in the direction I knew my house to be. My house, but not my *home*. Home was back in New York. Back where things were familiar and safe and real and I stumbled on stones, slid on the driveway, scraped my hands. Wet and stinging with blood. Remembering the old backyard: the grill I was always promising to clean, the cedar deck, the badminton net, the swing set.

But water still manages to seep in, doesn't it, Michael? Thought you filled the cracks, but you missed a few spots. A few *important* spots. And now the space between solid meaning are widening. Not much (not yet at least) but enough to tell. Enough to drive you crazy. No way you can ignore it now.

I ran up the front steps, to the door, standing there and shivering though the night was warm. Still found it hard to breathe. Suffocating. Gasping for air. Still in the coffin, buried without hope, pushing at the lid. No give. Pounding at the lid.

No way out. No air. Can't—

Before I could reach out and turn the knob, the door swung inward on its own and impossible, miraculous light flooded my grave.

"Honey, what's wrong?" Moira asked, standing there at the threshold.

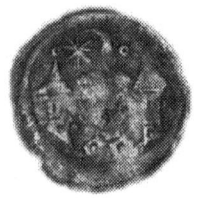

seventeen

"The woman who drove the pickup fell asleep."

It didn't matter that it was Pete speaking to me that afternoon. Didn't matter who the hell it was. He didn't have to come straight out and tell me. As he spoke, I could see it all. Both Moira and Jeni after the accident, their bodies mangled. I asked if I needed to do anything like identify the bodies. Pete said, gently, that there was nothing much left to identify. I would never see their faces again.

In horrible dream-flashes, I'd see them lying in the road in pieces, mauled, glass from the honeycombed windshield scattered in their remains like diamonds—rubies where the blood had pooled. But Pete was wrong. I could tell who they were. My imagination would not let me off so easily. I'd see their sightless eyes and know. Know the unfairness, know the pain and hate everything and everyone—most of all myself for not being there to save them. But I could never know. Could never reclaim that lost day.

But *you* could have driven Jeni to the dentist! Why didn't you, Mr. Mike? Moira went ahead and took off work while you were sitting around at home. What would it have cost you to get up from that stupid typewriter and take an hour of your precious time——

We had an argument.

Who?

Moira and I.

What about?

Well... I was working on an important part of a new novel and was giving it all my attention——

And?

Moira said she was busy, too.

So...

She conceded. Told me she'd pick up Jeni, take her there and bring her back.

All so you could write. Great excuse. Wonderful. I wonder what words (so high and mighty) you were writing when their lives ended? Or maybe you weren't even writing, hm? Maybe you took a break and turned on the TV, or went to get something to eat, or went to the bathroom——

Jesus Christ, will you just stop!

Why? It's never going to end. You can't use words this time, Mike. This time you've got to meet things head on.

Yet there I stood, in the doorway of my new house, with Moira before me. She had no bruises. Her eyes were beautiful. Losing myself in them.

"Moira?"

Her face took on a look of worried urgency and her voice was frayed with concern, "You look absolutely *ill!*"

This isn't right, I told myself. It's all wrong. So just stop. Stop playing the mind games. I know it's you. You're doing this. It looks and sounds like her, but it's only a mental ruse. It wants me to see her. Wants me to touch her. Wants me to believe she's not really dead.

But that was wrong, too. I didn't want this, did I? I didn't start this game. Didn't tell it to begin like all the others. I knew it would hurt. This isn't me. This is something else entirely.

"Come on," she said, taking me by the arm, "Dinner's almost ready. I'll fix you a drink and bring it out."

Moving into the living room not as in a dream, but perfect reality—if such a thing could ever truly exist. The entire room was different. I thought at first I was in some other house, this woman someone else's wife... But it was only the furnishing—the room was the same as before, though nowhere near as empty. Three identical sofas ringed an octagonal table of some dark wood. A copy of Better Homes rested upon it, opened to an advertisement for sinks and bathtubs. And everything was warm. So warm...

"Be right back," she said, sitting me down onto the middle sofa and disappearing through the archway into the kitchen. It was then that I noticed the smell. Chicken. Moira's baked lemon-pepper chicken. The light was low—served only by two small decorative lamps on either side of me. In some other room (the kitchen? dining room?) familiar music drifted through. It wasn't until I focused on it that I realized it was the Eagles. Then someone appeared behind me in the archway.

A frail whisper: "Daddy?"

My daughter raced into my arms, just out of the bath and in her pajamas, hair damp, cheeks flushed. Her eyes, however, were heavy. Tears wandered behind them. Again, I felt it: wrongness.

"Why were you gone so long?" she asked.

A question I should have asked her.

Why?

Because they're not real.

Yes, they are.

In your mind. All in your mind.

"Daddy, I thought you weren't coming back," and then she began to sob. I helped her into my lap and wiped her tears.

See! She's real! You can't say she's not!

But how——?

But just then it didn't matter. I shut the voices out. Didn't matter if she was real or not. She was there. Now. With me. In my arms. Snuggling closer, tiny head on my shoulder. I held her and, eventually, she calmed.

I found it nearly impossible to speak. I could open my mouth fine, could move my lips as well, but past this I couldn't get a single word out. And then her eyes. Staring up at me as they always used to. Brown, like her mother's.

Shaking, I was somehow able to speak. My words seemed distant. "I'm here," I told her, "I'm not going away."

Her tears came again, choked with words:

"I had a dream, Daddy. And you went away forever. And me and Mommy were really sad."

I felt tears, and they wanted out.

Push 'em back, now's not the time.

"Mommy said you weren't ever coming back. That you could *never* come back."

"I'm here now, Sweetie," was all I could manage. I don't even think she heard me.

Carefully, she put her arms around my neck and sat up a bit straighter. Slowly, a smile, though slight, began to form at the ends of her lips. So fragile.

She said, "Sing for me, Daddy?"

And I could no longer hold back the tears.

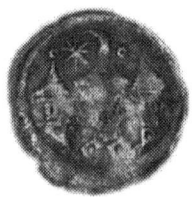

eighteen

Imagine sitting beneath a tree with the sun hidden somewhere above—you don't know exactly where it is, but there's light. Secondary light. This is the light I now moved in, or more precisely, floated *through*. Jeni had gone off to bed. I wanted to go with her, tuck her in, but knew if I even moved my emotions would overload. She padded off and blended in with all those other shadows, a grey and inconstant outline up the stairway.

A new Eagles song replaced the old one, "The Sad Café."

Moira shuffled quickly in, humming along with it and handed me a cold drink. I thought, suddenly, so that's how they did it! My water may not have been poisoned, but they put something in it, some hallucinogen, to make me think this all was real! But then (still floating in the light) did it really matter? Moira was here with me, now, my love...

The ice clinked hollowly in the glass as I raised it for a sip. My stomach was furious. I wanted a taste of that chicken *now*. Tired of waiting. But the drink was simply heaven: Sprite on the rocks. Moira brushed the back of my neck with her hand and disappeared again into the kitchen.

When I knew she was gone, I downed the drink in one long swallow. Chewed the ice. Turned off the lamp to my right and set the empty glass on the dark, parquet table.

You know this place, don't you?

Yes, I knew it. As if I'd sat in this very seat every evening for the past ten or eleven years. I felt strangely comfortable on the couch. Familiar with it. Looking across the room and seeing the small clock on the fireplace mantle— knowing it, too. I recalled buying the thing, setting it there at the inspection of both wife and daughter. A little bit to the left... little more... now to the right... *There!* Perfect!

The carpet, however, still smelled new. Not yet worn in. Such intimacy inside an alien "unknown".

"Moira?" I called.

"Almost ready," she answered, "Did you put Jeni to bed?"

Yeah, I thought, just like old times.

Slowly, I rose. At the kitchen archway, the music grew slightly louder. So many shadows. I walked in. Even the kitchen light was low. Moira stood over the stove and was now singing, no longer humming. She turned to me, smiling the way she always used to smile. Without a word, she gestured to the open door of the dining room. I couldn't help but return the smile, forever lost in a world that should never have been. Taking my cue, I left her to finish, though feared I'd never see her again. That she'd simply vanish, as quick and without warning as she had the first time.

I entered the dining room and felt safe (and miserable and lonely and afraid) and wanted to run down the disjointed paths in the woods again. Then I was happy I was home and wanted to scream and cry and finally sat down at the table.

There were two wine glasses beside two sets of china and silverware. A small chandelier gave light, but it seemed so high above. Too high. A star, not the sun. Distant and surreal, where everything around and between and beyond is the dusty freeze of space. Light years here were only the faintest of breaths in the depths of sleep. Dizzy, I looked down again into the glass. I watched light spiral in its curvature. Downward, forever down; terrible water-spout. The glass took me in circles and I felt myself falling.

"Here we go," Moira announced, wearing a pair of light blue oven mitts, carrying to the table a platter heavy with baked lemon-pepper chicken.

My mouth watered; my eyes did as well.

She disappeared once more, returning again with a dish of potatoes. Repeating the act one last time, she reappeared with a small basket of fresh rolls and bottle of wine. I pulled the chair out for her and received another smile. "Always the gentleman," she commented softly. I found my own seat.

"You know," Moira began, "I wasn't sure if you'd make it." She paused, blushing slightly, "I just didn't think you could, that's all."

I was looking into her eyes the entire time. In peripheral, I tore small pinches from the warm bread and collected them on my plate. I tasted one of the pieces, as fine as ever. "I don't know," she continued, "I'm just glad you're here."

But where *was* here?

I wasn't home, no matter how comfortable I felt. Actually, I felt just as comfortable as uncomfortable. I reached for the wine bottle (Louis de Camponac red Bordeaux) and poured for both of us. A silent toast left me spinning. I sipped the chilled liquid (incredible), then peered through the amber waves at Moira. Her face shifted impossibly. A bizarre look back in time to the accident.

I set the glass down and quickly took her hands in mine, mainly to stop my own from shaking.

"I don't know what's going on," I stammered, "but I can't stand this anymore. I've always needed you, but now... now I know *how* much I need you." Her hand so real. Her skin... I rose from my chair and knelt down beside her, brought her hand to my lips. Looked up. "I couldn't stand to lose you again. Jeni was acting so strange before—"

"Jeni? How?"

"I don't know; she seemed... distant."

Moira pushed away from the table and started for the kitchen. I followed: through the house and up the stairs, turning right, second room on the left. She pushed the door in and her face went blank. The room was empty. No toys. No boxes of hand-me-down play clothes. No Disney bed-sheets. No warmth. As the house had been before.

Before what?

Before your dead wife and daughter decided to show up, Mr. Mike. C'mon! Get with the program!

And then Jeni seemed no longer a part of this alternate reality.

The escape, simply, was Moira. My arm around her shoulder. To feel her there beside me. A solid and real thing. There it is again... that word. *Real.*

"I'm tired," she said, turning toward me, draping her arms around my neck. I picked her gently up and walked down toward the other end of the hallway. Recognizing the Indian wall-hanging, the picture of the sea... She snuggled closer, her tender cheek against my neck. A sigh. She was my lost treasure.

Please, this isn't fair. Why do I feel so awful? This is what I wanted, isn't it? To have her back?

It's also what I feared more than anything. My life, in my arms, my dreams, my love. The door to the master bedroom was open, but all I could see through the space between was darkness. The light had been on before, though, hadn't it? Sure. Wasn't imagining that.

"I'll get it," Moira said, reaching out with her right arm

and pouring on the light. Pushing the door in further, I found the room beautiful, though smaller than it had seemed before when it was empty. The most stunning feature was the bed, an enormous canopy bed. A bed that, as was everything else, something I knew and knew well.

But you never lived here!

I know, but—

You never slept here!

I *know,* it's just—

Damnit, listen to yourself! You can't do this! You can't possibly believe this is really happening, can you? Don't put yourself through it. Don't do it.

Walking to the bed, I set her down as I myself leaned into the mattress. The covers seemed to melt with our weight and all that remained in my world was the complete bliss of the woman I loved. My wife. My everything. I held her and believed again in all I'd given up on. Believed that the impossible was no longer beyond me. And at the same time I felt her slipping away. The closer we were, the stronger I felt she was truly lost.

Half-in, half-out of the covers, we watched one another. Lost in her beauty. We held each other and her hair smelled as it always had when she'd shower just before bed, after a long day at the hospital. Her skin was slightly moist and I kissed her shoulder.

"I'm so glad you're finally here," she whispered, as if we'd been separated not by days, but decades. Her words were soft on me. Her breath: just as sweet. I kissed her again. Her hand barely touched my cheek. Nothing else, nothing at all mattered.

The light above seemed magically to flicker out, a dying taper, all oxygen depleted.

She whispered, "Love me."

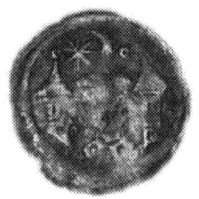

nineteen

tick!

   tick!

Through my mind this incessant tapping, weaving from the sleep-world into the real and back again, growing louder with each pass. Stronger. I reached for Moira, opened my eyes, but found only the cold, wood-plank floor beneath me. I looked around.

Nothing.

tick!

A stale, warm breeze through the open bedroom doorway.

Everything as it had been. Empty. Without substance.

tick!

I wanted to scream. Scream and never stop because how wonderful it would be to stop thinking, only the ringing in my ears and my burning throat... But I couldn't scream.

Couldn't open my mouth. All I saw was the empty bedroom smear before me through a flood of hot, stinging tears, the sunlight bending and warping, reaching, maniacal tendrils with a mind of their own, wanting only to wrap themselves around me. If only they could pull me through the window! Into the morning to keep me warm! I waited for this, my loss an overwhelming force that pushed in at every direction both physical and emotional, but the tendrils only fell away. Left me stranded. Melted.

tick!

I managed to sit, my entire body aching. My shoulder felt like set concrete—it hurt to turn, to move my neck.

tick! tick!

Where was that damn sound coming from?

I managed to stand up, though wanted to fall back down, through the floor, through the ground. The wood, however, would not allow me to slip through.

Why not? It did last night.

But that was different.

How?

It wasn't just a dream.

Then what was it?

tick!

The sound was now more than simply a gentle tap. In all its calmness, it found a way to smash at my head.

Tick!

Each time with growing strength.

I looked down at the floor and found the planks coated with hardly a rime of dust. Except, that is, in four circular areas. Circles that had been the feet of the canopy bed.

Tick! Tick!

It happened without my conscious awareness. A snap-shutter succession of movement that led me downstairs toward the den.

In the hall. No tapestry. No picture of the sea. Staring momentarily at footprints that had molded themselves in the new carpet. TICK! At the bottom of the stairs. Standing in the center of the living room. Boxes. TICK! No sofa. No mantelpiece clock. TICK! The kitchen faucet ran freely, the drain plugged with wet paper towels. Water cascaded freely onto the linoleum. A puddle. A stream.

TICK!

A river.

On the door of the fridge were some pictures. Scenes from a coloring book. I recognized them all.

Jeni's.

TICK!

Standing in the den... my proposed haven where I was to write. Empty, but for my cot and the typewriter which was now propped on a few of the smaller boxes. A sheet of paper sat in the rollers.

TICK! TICK! said the machine and I watched as the keys appeared magically to bounce through the alphabet; I tore the sheet out and stared at the words that greeted me:

THEY'RE BOTH IN HELL

And Marsh's voice in my mind:

"You can't leave Hell."

And a rising fear that I was going to die. I don't know from where it came, or why it was there, but it would not go away. I couldn't decide if I wanted it to go or stay. I started shaking, felt vulnerable just standing there, needed to *move*. The room was closing in.

In one last shutter-click, I found myself standing before Marsh's front door. The morning shocked me. I'd expected something overcast, something dark and heavy and grey. Something that spat tepid raindrops. Instead, the sun beamed happily in a chalcedonic sky. A breeze both soothing and warm; the after-storm, post-evening scent of green, of trees and grass and wet-but-aerating clay. I took in a long breath and made it last. It felt so good and so wrong. My hair clung to my scalp annoyingly, my mouth thick and pasty, my clothes loose on my frame. I felt used, a wash-rag rung out once too often, stained and torn. I opened the door (didn't bother knocking) and entered the soupy darkness. In the living room, all monitors were on, blinking silently with numbers, giving the room artificial life as shadows jumped and shook and shifted in the alternating light. All was silent. Marsh was nowhere.

I called his name.

No answer.

Examining the screens more closely, I discovered a strange succession of words meshed together as one, scrolling, over and over, never stopping. It was difficult to make them out:

PRYIPHLEGETHONCOCYTUSLETHENETHERLA
MNEMOSGNETARTARUSACHERONCASTALIAIS
LANDOFTHEBLESSEDSTYXAEACUSAELYSIAN

And my mind spun with each of them.

"Marsh? Marshall!" I shouted. Still, no response. I looked at another computer, another screen:

HELPMEDADDYHELPMEMICHAELHELPMEDADDY

"Marsh!"

Next to one of the screens were those damn foil packets and loose capsules. I pocketed them and moved out of the living room—down toward the kitchen. The room was dark. When I threw the switch, I found half the cabinets open and disgorged. The water-faucet was on and running. The sink here, too, was clogged. Another stream.

So many rivers.

The table was littered with ripped-open bags of sour-cream and onion chips, disgraced with empty cans of the omnipresent A&W, but Marsh was nowhere.

Back in the hall, I turned a corner (to the right) and

nearly tripped over him. His eyes like wet glass, open and watching the dark ceiling above. His mouth and lips were firmly set, bluish. Not a smile, really, but instead an ironic look of understanding.

His cheeks were bloated, as if he'd just finished eating an entire bag of chips, but when I knelt down, I realized that something of definite proportion and solidity waited behind them. Slightly sickened by the act, though at the same time intrigued, I parted his dry lips and pulled from his mouth a small handful of coins. Old coins. There were three of them, each quite heavy and I put them in my pocket with the capsules.

I thought again of losing Moira and Jeni and with a jolt was sobered. Not much, I suppose, but enough. I tried not to allow my feelings to slow me. They, instead, urged me on. I tried to remember the conversations I'd had with Marsh not so long ago. He'd known Dr. Brace. Worked with him and others from the University. I reached into my pocket and touched the pen. MCWHORTER FUNERAL HOME. What Pete had to do with this I had no idea, except that he was definitely involved. He somehow knew Marsh and Dr. Brace and a great number of people (including me) from a place and time in our past. But why? And what of Weatherstone?

Marsh staring upward.

Me looking down.

The sound of running water from the kitchen. I hadn't bothered turning off the faucet in my own kitchen, nor did I bother here.

"What now, Marsh?" I asked in a soft whisper.

There was no response.

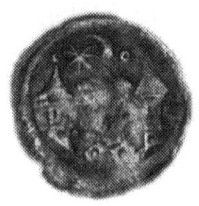

twenty

I'd left the keys under the front seat of the car and in one fluid motion scooped up the brass ring that bound them, turned over the ignition and threw the rental into gear. The sun was suddenly furious with me, sending spiteful peals of fire through the windshield; it was near impossible to see. I'd had a pair of sunglasses, but couldn't remember where I left them—turned the blinders down, both of them, but they only seemed to reduce my visibility further.

Turning a circle in the cul-de-sac, I picked up speed down Blackberry Way.

The sun was higher now (out of sight above the roof) yet no less merciful. My eyes watered in the heat. Even with the windows open, the late-morning air blowing in my face, I still felt burdened with the sweat that soaked my neck and back. My shirt was drenched.

Clouds of particulate clay and soil plumed behind me, settling slowly again to the ground. I reached blindly under the passenger's seat: nothing. A quick glance into the back seats: nothing.

Suddenly, I was at the crossroads and put all my weight on the brakes. The car fishtailed then stopped in a chaotic disturbance of dust.

I could still picture Marsh in my mind, though he wasn't staring at the ceiling. His eyes were fierce, penetrating and as painful as the sun. I couldn't blink him away. Couldn't lose the image.

Waiting.

For the dust.

To clear.

I clicked open the glove compartment and my sunglasses slid out onto the floor. Donning them, I squinted as the sign dissolved from the orange film of silt and clay.

SWEETWATER

LA VISTA   WEATHERSTONE
BLACKBERRY   PHASE TWO

I took the left toward La Vista. Five-hundred feet later, the road dead-ended to nothing more than scrub. I drove back and turned right toward Phase Two. Another dead-end about a mile down.

I expected the same from the road to Weatherstone, prepared myself for another disappointment, but instead found myself before a ten-foot high hurricane fence topped with a coiled stitching of razor wire. The fence ran out of sight in both directions, slowly curving inward on the hill it enclosed. I could see there was no entrance gate. No way in.

On the other side of the fence was an expanse of grassy field rising steadily upward. At the top, a polished opal, waited

Weatherstone. A sterile, white building resembling a hospital or clinic. Few windows. Entirely impersonal.

The answers were there. I *knew* they were there. If I could just get past this barrier... Not only was the fence tall, but the poles were set to lean outward (toward me) at a substantial angle. Also, I hadn't half the strength required to scale it. My body was sprung, my mind flying on extremes of high and low.

I turned the car around, backing up a good fifty feet. If it had been my own car, I would have thought no more of it. Then I thought about the person who had killed Moira and Jeni. Were their thoughts as desperate as mine? Did they want to kill my family as much as I wanted to puncture this fence?

The woman was sleeping at the wheel, for cryin' out loud!

That's only what Pete had said.

She wanted to kill them, some part of me replied.

Don't be ridiculous.

I felt filthy for harboring such thoughts. The fence would go down. I had no doubt of it. I'd go through or be destroyed.

Letting my foot quickly off the clutch, I threw all my weight on the gas. There was no slow-motion this time. No stop-shutter photography. It happened all at once. It happened with speed. And the fence was soft butter to my dull, warm knife. Might as well have been that beautiful woman and child. Might as well have been them, not the fence, not the steel, but bone; not sleeping pills, but hatred and anger and blind insanity.

I broke through! Didn't stop. Racing up the hill, the car bucked and pitched in all directions. There was no way to manage the sinkholes. Just go through them.

Half-way up the hill I braked. I still needed the car to take me back and didn't feel like risking a blow-out or some other eventuality. I let the car stall and pulled the keys half-out of the ignition, letting them hang.

I didn't look back. Didn't inspect the mess at the bottom of the hill that might have been stiffening flesh/steel. In the end, it was all the same. Didn't matter. The answers were forward, not backward. Still tired and breathing heavily with each step, I progressed methodically upward to the base of the building. The front doors were of thick, tinted glass: black. I could see nothing beyond. Didn't matter. Nothing mattered. Just get in!

I pulled on the door handle. Locked.

Shouldn't there be a guard? Some sort of security?

Stupidly, I knocked.

A hollow knock. Strange, with an echo.

I knocked again. Dull and empty.

My reflection stared back at me and I saw how skeletal I looked. Sallow eyes, sunken deep. My face was drawn. Someone else on the other side of the door, not I. That couldn't be me.

Sorry, Mr. Mike, can't get off that easy. It's only you. You and the pit you've fallen into.

Fallen? I was *pushed!*

So find out who stood behind you, then. See who did the pushing.

I hit the door at the frame and it rattled; the sound echoed as did my knocking. Frustrated, I began to circumnavigate the structure; solid, white stone as I moved along. The grass was not grass, but crabby weeds at my feet. No landscape artisan had been on the company's payroll, that was for sure.

Is this where Marsh had come for his drugs?

At the end of the front face of the building, I slowly turned the corner, hoping to discover a side entrance—a maintenance door.

There were no doors. No alternate entrance. Where the building should have been, it was not. All I could see were massive rows of support beams holding the one-dimensional facade upright. I felt as if I were on a movie set, just stepping out of camera-shot and breaking the fictional dream. I felt cheated and angry.

There was a wind on the hill that blew into my shirt, causing it to ruffle. A cool wind. I closed my eyes and savored it. When it was gone, as all good things find themselves, I looked across the hills beyond and could just make out the two houses that were Marsh's and my own. Monopoly houses, they seemed (more props in this movie set) and stretched out beyond were the woods I'd lost more than my way in. It would have been interesting to see all that land as I now saw the houses: small, inconsequential, toys, an electric-train landscape, but the dark forest of fluid paths and frozen rivers were no less magnificent. No less menacing. It all seemed somehow larger, even *more* threatening from a distance.

Another breeze coursed up the hill, pushing wildly at the building with no doors.

No answers.

The wind pushed stupidly, not knowing what else to do.

It knew my name.

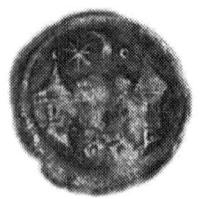

twenty-one

I twisted the key time and again, but the car would not turn over. I made my way downhill, urged on by the soft sound of the wind as it pushed against me. The sky bid itself a shade darker as clouds crept determinedly in. Important things now seemed not to matter and I found myself fascinated with the trivial. Abandoning the rental, I became obsessed with my walk to the gaping fence below; for some reason, I decided that this had to be accomplished in a perfectly straight line. Each time I stumbled, I tried my hardest to recover the initial course of travel. I started counting my steps as well, guessing how many more it would take to reach the fence. One hundred? No, somewhere around one-twenty. And what about back to the house? Two-thousand? Three? I counted the sinkholes, too. By the time I had reached the fence: sixty-three holes and 237 steps.

I turned back, staring up at the building that wasn't. Someone had gone through a lot of time and trouble to induce this illusion. The question sill remained: who?

And why? The wind: stronger. Choking clouds of dust rose from the road and I found myself walking blindly, feeling my way about with tired feet, eyes stinging. My trance grew heavier here, for I remembered nothing of the remaining walk to the house. Just that it was dark... and I stood there staring out the kitchen window—out into the amorphous, shifting shadows of the backyard. All that was left of daylight had concentrated at the horizon, a thin film of dusty, blue light. The woods comprised a singular entity, undulating to a primordial, genetic clock. A veritable sea, the tree-tops swayed in groups that were waves and swelled and tossed foam. The tide would crash at the bottom of the hill far below and I could hear the fury even from where I stood. From the distance, yet not so far away: a heavy volley of thunder. This was the eternal surf. I thought back to my childhood at the Jersey Shore. Of falling asleep in a tiny bungalow with all the windows open and if I listened hard enough I could hear the distant surf. The Atlantic Ocean sat not two hundred feet away. I always seemed to be afraid. Afraid the waves would creep silently up and carry me away, but I didn't dare close the windows! If that were the case, I would never hear their stealthy approach. It was better to have at least some advantage. True, the open windows allowed for easy access to a young boy, but what would I do if I did make it out the window?

The water would pour in nonetheless, moving me along as easily it did the cars and other small houses, making driftwood of what had been life, not particularly interested in consequence.

Now, the waves were not so shy. They announced their arrival without reproach. Closer. No stars above. No fire. Moldering darkness. No means of judging direction, location, position; spun in circles with a blindfold. Imbalanced.

Still spinning.

How did I feel at that moment, aside from the turmoil I watched helplessly below? I wasn't angry anymore... I wasn't annoyed, though I felt I should have been. I suppose I was scared. Afraid, maybe, because I knew sooner or later I'd have to go down there. I'd have to do something, preferably sooner than later. If I didn't at least try, I don't think I'd ever be close to the person I left behind in that other, Northern world. That person was gone, but the important parts of him still made occasional appearances. At the very least, I'm proof of that.

I rubbed the coarse stubble on my chin against the collar of my shirt. My mind suddenly sailed at a thought: she was still there! Still there and I thought she'd finally left for good. The shampoo Moira had just used—mixed with the hint of baby powder—still clung to me, to my shirt. If I closed my eyes (which I did) and imagined (which wasn't so hard) I could still feel her head resting on my shoulder. Sense her breath on my neck. Hear her heartbeat.

Thunder.

The sheets and blankets on the bed the previous night had held us aloft, in the clouds, protected. After we'd made love, after she'd fallen asleep, I held her, not wanting to succumb to sleep. Not wanting to give up what I feared would soon be taken.

In the morning, I almost expected what I was left with. Only the cold floor and bitter sorrow I'd grown to expect of the morning.

In a steadily rising crescendo: *thunder*.

Then a fleeting strobe of hot purple on the distant hills, with echoes off the clouds.

The day was gone and I could survey the post-crepuscular landscape only in retrospect of lightning. Lightning which grew increasingly more frequent.

I took the pen from my pocket.

Read the familiar words.

What if—?

It didn't make sense...

What?

You know damn well what!

Yet still I could not dispel the notion. It had come up before. It would not go away. If Pete was the reason behind this (as I now hesitatingly believed he was) then Moira and Jeni might still be alive.

Alright, stop. You're kidding me, right?

No, think about it. You never actually saw their bodies, right?

Let's not go through this again—

And you didn't even go to the funeral. What if it all was a set-up?

A set-up? Get real! Next thing you'll be bringing Russian spies into the story.

But what if they really are alive?

You don't give up, do you? Okay, then. Why? For what purpose would they still be alive? Think! You're making excuses (empty excuses) and if you don't stop you just might convince yourself again. Then you'll fall. You'll fall like before, except this time you may not be able to stand back up. This time the fall won't end.

It didn't make sense, I knew that, but still I could not totally discount the possibility.

THEY'RE BOTH IN HELL

Recalling this message from earlier in the den, I shuddered. They're both in Hell: Moira and Jeni. It could be in reference to no one else. I'd been falling steadily since their departure, not holding my arms out to stop, just falling and making it worse. New York to South Carolina. Falling. My new house down the steep backyard and into the choking forest. Falling. Falling...

Still falling.

It was going to pour at any moment. It was going to

fall hard. I had no umbrella. Nor a jacket. I walked out onto the back deck, closing the sliding glass door behind me.

You don't have to do this. Just—

Just what? Go to my cot and fall asleep? Sure, I'd get plenty of sleep tonight. Or maybe I should bring the damn cot upstairs and maybe when I wake up it won't be a cot anymore, but a canopy bed.

Sorry. Can't quite get that one down.

Standing at the verge of the deck, I stared down at the tips of my sneakers, flush with a seven foot drop—and most probably a four-hundred foot roll further down the hill. The wind was much stronger now.

A raindrop.

Just one.

Then more wind. Heavy thunder: in my feet, in my soul. Roaring deep and telling lies I believed because—

Lightning cracked above me, splitting heavy granite clouds. Sending it all down, my own private show. And so I dove in.

Down wood-plank steps. Down the weedy, stone-clotted hill. Down into the ocean that wasn't an ocean, yet everything a body of water was supposed to be. The undulant branches and thorns that lapped this false shore began to pull. The tide grew heavier. More thunder. The undertow wanted no more than to take me in. So I allowed it.

I was nothing more than a cork in a dark and uncharted sea.

I was home.

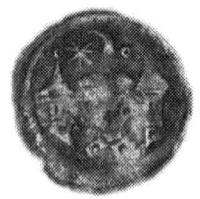

twenty-two

Lost.

I had absolutely no idea where I was going, yet allowed myself to be led forward. It happened slowly, but the "eyes" returned, boring into me, pulling me onward. Pushing me. My mind a buoy. The rain pulsing down.

In one great detonation, a spasm of lightning tore through the air a few hundred feet before me. The stench of charred wood and ozone grew more pungent with each step. Overwhelming. When I finally reached the area, chips of pine littered the forest floor in profusion. White ribbons of smoke rose against the pouring rain from the severed tree, creating the illusion of stillness; two forces working against one another and getting nowhere and I noticed something strange amidst the destruction.

Thunder.

The ground shook as if something beneath it strained

for release. Attached to a dismembered limb of the pine that had been hit, I discovered a curious silver box. But it wasn't a box, not really. Looking closer... a camera and small speaker similar to the kind I'd seen in Tiny Peco's. The lens was cracked and a length of thin wire ran from it to the end of the pine branch—then terminated, for it had apparently been torn in the fall.

I looked up, into the swaying trees, and was able to pick out several similar cameras bobbing to and fro in the wind. Here were my "eyes". I wasn't crazy!

But why the little speakers? I don't remember hearing anything. As a matter of fact, I'd heard nothing at all. Not a sound.

Are you sure?

I toyed briefly with the thought of subliminal persuasion, messages that might have been given to me without my knowledge, but why? I wasn't involved in any government cover-up or scandal. Why all this secrecy and high-tech delusion?

The rain continued to fall. Harder. Hot, thick needles bleeding through my clothes, my skin. I continued on, following nothing but an indefinable, intangible line of rope some part of me seemed tethered to. A life-line, or should I be so foolish to think so?

Through the trees, which lashed out at me.

Thunder.

Heavenly lights turning the landscape an alternating positive-negative.

Dead end. And all was slightly familiar. I still had a difficult time remembering the particulars of my last trip down here, but the dead end was a part of it. I knew it was. It was easier this time to pick out the rock formation before me. The trees pulled magically away to both sides, creating a disturbing pathway to the entrance of the cave.

THEY'RE BOTH IN HELL

I'd been thinking back on certain things—though not quite clearly. Muddy waters. I neared the aperture in the stone and stared into the dark void that willingly accepted the onslaught of rain.

First, I went back to my college years, my first meeting with Pete. Though I was undecided about my career, one thing (except writing) kept my interest long enough for me to pursue a list of classes which eventually led to major in English. These classes were all in Mythology and Classical Literature. I ate the stuff up. Couldn't get enough of it. I went beyond the call of duty when it came to papers on the subject. I researched until I exhausted every source.

So here were the rivers. The freezing current of the first I'd discovered would be the river Cocytus. The second river, which seemed to have caused me to forget much of what had happened: the river Lethe. And then there was the message on the screen in Marsh's living room, naming not only the remaining rivers of the Underworld, but those provinces which divided them. Still, it made no sense! How could it possibly be true? But it was!

Then: how did Pete fit into everything?

Perhaps he discovered all this and brought me down here to say good-bye.

Good-bye to whom?

Who do you think?

You can't be serious.

Why not? There's some good in it, isn't there?

Tell me, then, what good has come of all this so far? Are you glad you were able to see Moira and Jeni again last night? No good-byes, Mr. Mike. Only hopes, and wishes. Impossibilities.

I was getting close. Close to making the choice I feared making. Feared because I already knew what my answer would be.

I could turn back—not so hard, just go back and leave Sweetwater (whatever the hell Sweetwater was) and walk until someone found it in their heart to pick up a distraught traveler. Walk until my head was clear. Until I found enough strength to call Pete and get things straight once and for all.

Or—?

Or I could take that first step down into the rain-slick cave entrance.

Why?

At first there was no answer. Merely standing there. Hoping a more plausible reason would rise before me. Which didn't happen. I knew how much it would hurt, yet I wanted to see them again. Needed to see them. Last night was a drug and I needed more, to hold onto what was gone. It was all a trick. A trick inside my mind. I stopped trying to figure out what was wrong with me. Whatever it was, I was far beyond rational thought.

I took a step forward.

Another.

Going down was easier this time. Pressed between the rock walls like slimy, wet clay. I pushed further. Harder. I began to conform—still a bolus of Earth—to the passage. Then, finally, I was free as the wall opened, thrown to the cold and rainy bottom.

Beyond a turn in the cave fell light. Beautiful, violet-tinged light. The night-light outside my bedroom door.

But don't close the door, not all the way... there, just like that so the light falls through just enough to color the walls and rouge the darkness.

I crawled toward it on hands and knees. The light grew stronger.

My hands slipped often on the wet stone. I'd been here before, but what waited around the wall of stone? Beyond the turn? What offered such light?

Pressing down upon me: that feeling again. Eyes, yes, but much more. I looked around, but could find not a single camera, nothing except the cool and sweaty rock, and the light.

On shaky knees, I stood.

One careful, metered step. After that I couldn't seem to go on. A pure, icy fear leaked into my heart and in turn pulsed through my arteries; an injection of some foreign poison designed to terrorize and incapacitate.

Thunder echoed deafeningly throughout the cave, resounding with a subtle sub-bass that heightened a rising doubt. Whispers in my mind. Then my thoughts cleared for one, brief moment and I remembered Marsh's medication. I took the foil packet from my pocket and pushed out two of the blue capsules. Swallowed one.

How strong were they?

Remember Marsh's eyes...?

Sure, but how many had he taken?

A minute passed. I felt nothing.

Downed another capsule.

After a moment, the light beyond began slowly to sharpen, the fuzz leaving the edges. Something was different. Whatever was in the capsule was definitely some sort of stimulant, as I had hoped. My mind now artificially fine-tuned, I took in my surroundings more carefully. Blood drummed in my ears. Pounding. Louder. And something strange happened. I no longer found myself scared. I didn't fear rounding the corner of the cave. The light bore no malice.

I was, instead, angry. *Furious.* I pocketed the empty foil packet and moved on, around the turn, out of the cave and to the bank of a river. The river I'd visited not long ago. I remembered drinking. But how could I have done so? Looking down into it, the water appeared grey, murky, pouring from a crack in a stone wall far to my left. It looked no less quenching than a glass of wet chalk.

Something else was different as well. When last I'd visited, I remembered heavy fog on the opposite bank of the river.

The river Lethe, right Mr. Mike? You're the in

Underworld now. Ha, ha.

But I couldn't lead myself entirely to a solid conclusion on that as yet.

The sound of bells. Heavy bells. Thick and mellow, growing louder.

Closer.

With the mist gone, I could see far into the distance— as if I weren't below the Earth, but in the valley of an ancient mountain. Great tendrils of mist swirled high above, clinging to the ceiling, creating the illusion of clouds. I moved further down the bank, the rush of water growing exponentially louder with each step.

Also rising, the song of the bell.

As the land began to fall, Lethe joined several other tributaries to form one, great river. My footing began to deteriorate. The thick, muddy ground sucked at my feet, threatening to steal my sneakers and socks and leave me barefoot. I moved carefully along the bank and soon enough the land leveled out. The scent of asphodel made me sick it was so overwhelming. The flowers ran rampant all around. I followed them to a copse of trees behind me. Poplars, they were. Black poplars and willows. The illusion of an open atmosphere was almost completely believable now and for a moment I forgot about the solid sky and limited horizon that now ruled my world.

Cautiously, I approached the trees. Once in their shade, I immediately wondered where the light was coming from. There certainly was no sun or moon, no daylight. It was evening in the land above, and with storm. As if to reconfirm this, thunder from a forgotten world rocked the soil on which I stood.

I felt the drug dig further into me with black fingers, slick and scaly. My thoughts flowed freely and with great speed; quick and powerful visions filled my head. I kept seeing my typewriter. Sitting before it, typing out the words to a novel whose main character finds himself in Hades, searching for those things lost, foremost himself.

But it wasn't a novel. Nor fiction. Whatever was happening, however it was happening, was a pseudo-reality.

The bells calling to me from the mist-ensconced shore of the great Acheron, the river of sorrow and lamentation. The river of affliction. The river of sadness.

I was already deep into the trees. Spanish moss grew freely here, traveling up the sides of the trees and sending down dark, verdant streamers. I had to stop from staring.

Despite my disorientation, I found the place painfully beautiful. A powerful thought then filled me: Moira should see this. She loved those pictures of old, southern plantation houses, moss dripping lazily from oaks and willows and eaves alike.

But Moira's gone.

Or is she?

THEY'RE BOTH IN HELL

But isn't that where I am?

I glanced at my feet and noticed a pile of thin twigs. Kneeling, I was surprised to discover writing on them, though it was too dim to make the letters out. Scooping up a small handful, I squinted and managed to read: MCWHORTER FUNERAL HOME. Not sticks, but pens. Hundreds of them, all around me. The bells: closer, the trees swaying in the breeze. Breeze? Down here? I breathed deeply. The air was still redolent with asphodel, though now with something else as well. A dank, dead smell. Instead of cringing from it, I breathed even deeper. Wanted more of it.

Shaking, I walked back toward the river and watched a shape float slowly toward me. The bells again, and I knew now the shape that created the sound.

My hand opened and the pens fell out onto the muddy river-bank. A few went in head first and stuck out like rotting teeth. But this mouth was not silent, the teeth not salvageable. More whispers with foul breath and accusation. It wouldn't come any closer, though. Would not kiss with cracked and bloated lips. I brought my foot down, pushing the teeth through the mud until they were gone. No smile. No kiss.

The bells.

The water lapped softly, yet with greedy, hissing insistence at the shore.

And the shape, a few moments before so hazy and nondescript, now took on the vague form of a raft—a five-sided raft with a figure standing off to the left of it. It pushed the raft along with a knobby staff. Closer. Clad in a cassock and as small as a child.

Tied to this staff were the bells: some small, some large: copper and silver and tin and brass. The sound bounced from the water against the misty false-sky and back into the copse of trees. There in the vegetation, the sound died slowly, eaten patiently by the dark leaves and branches and moss. But there were always more bells to feed the starved silence. Certainly, no sunlight provided the needed energy to allow proper growth.

The wet, sour-meat stench grew bolder as the raft began to overtake the shore. If this were traditional Hades, then it was Charon now closing in on me; I could now more clearly discern his cloak and hood. I could not make out a face though, nor eyes. Nothing but its arms working the single oar.

With a soft *whump*, the raft landed on the river-bank.

The bells pealed with a sharp singularity. One Christmas, Moira and I had gotten Jeni a toy piano. It had only half an octave, but she played it incessantly, treating it as if it were a treasured Baby Grand. A few nights later, I woke to hear her in her room, plinking away at the plastic keys. Except it didn't sound at all like a piano—nor even a toy piano. It sounded like what I heard now, though I could never have known then, each tone chiming the hours which passed in mere seconds, tintinabulous in the clouds and hallway and water and house and the ferryman stopped and waited. I could not breathe. The stench was unbearable.

Cautiously, I stepped onto the raft, leaving the mud-soaked shore for firmer (though less sure) ground. The figure did not move. Only stood there. Waiting.

I took one hesitant step toward it. Still nothing.

The sweet, cloying breeze did nothing to dispel the rot. The stink fell in nauseous waves on the surf of a dead-tide. Seaweed and decomposing fish. At the same instant I wanted to say and believe it was all a farce (like the Weatherstone complex... remember how real *that* was?) but something inside kept reminding me that I was really standing there.

Perhaps I had died back up in New York. Maybe I died, but went on regardless, a ghost driving a rental car down a highway to the Underworld. I nearly laughed. Why all these excuses?

The ferryman reached out and opened his hand. Muddied hand. Stinking hand. Nothing said. I went into my pockets again and retrieved one of the coins I'd found in Marsh's mouth. It was once believed that when one died, a token of passage was required to pass from the land of the living. An *obol*. I gave my coin to the keeper of the gate of eternal night. The obol was traditionally placed into a corpse's mouth before burial.

I placed my coin into Charon's foul palm (there, I've said it, Charon, he's Charon, okay?) and pulled my hand quickly back. I recoiled this time not because of odor or fear, but from a flash of familiarity. Something I'd just seen clicked in the back of my mind. It was quick. Barely perceptible. What was it?

Even under the veil of the drug, I still felt my defenses nowhere near as strong as they had been before this entire nightmare. The figure pulled his oar high and pushed the raft back across the river. The mist coiled at my feet, rising higher—at my knees now. We moved as though through a cloud; I looked above and saw more of the mist. The bells clanged, more hours that were really faster beings. I suddenly felt sleepy. Sweat broke freely across my body. I stared at the ferryman in a trance, his arms pulsing up and down (a single, dead piston reanimated to exist in slow-motion) and the sound of the oar entering and leaving the stale water, and the bells, bells, bells.

I knew nothing of how long I'd been on the raft, but in time I could hear the water's wake on the opposite bank of Acheron, the river of woe. We'd just traversed the river and Charon began to slow our advance. His (its) sleeve pulled loose in an upstroke and the flash of familiarity once again struck me. A glint. A brightness.

Then I saw it more clearly, on the ferryman's wrist, obscured partially by a thin layer of dark, gauzy material: a watch. A golden wrist-watch. And my thoughts raced back to a moment in time not so many days ago when I first arrived in Sweetwater—greeting Benson Aldritch. His watch had caught my attention then, giving him away now. This Charon was of the same height and build as the man I'd met before.

So now the question: for what reason? Why the play-acting? Someone had gone through a lot of trouble to pull this thing off. Then my thoughts were on Pete again. In a fragmented revelation I began to find more holes and inconsistencies. They were all from the outset; I simply hadn't any reason to notice them until now.

I thought back on Pete's "talks" in the distant past, one-sided conversations where he would sermonize about answers, the true meaning of life. It all seemed so crazy. What could he possibly gain from increasing my torment? I was the last person who had the answers he was so ardently searching for.

To Pete, every book was important. Each page held some secret (hidden or blatant) and he felt he had the talent to decipher it all. Each day and night, on vacations, continuously he sat himself before texts in the campus library. I saw him only when he wanted to be seen, knocking or calling when he needed temporary release from his studies. Strange how only until now I'd accepted it all as just idiosyncrasy and nothing more.

Above, once again, thunder reminded.

I was getting off track... the drugs?

Or was it me?

The ferryman (not ferryman... *Aldritch!*) motioned for me to step off the platform and onto the other shore. I did, but felt strange in doing so. What if I couldn't get back across the river and into the land of the living?

But it's not real!

Says who?

Then grab Charon's hood! Rip it off and unmask the fake for who he is!

So I stepped back onto the raft and advanced on the small figure. No more than two feet from him, I froze.

Do it! See what it all means!

But I couldn't. Couldn't do a damn thing. The watch was obscured again. Perhaps I was mistaken.

But you saw it!

Just imagined it.

My mind was spinning once again.

Maybe the drugs you took were spiked with something else to drive you insane!

But there's no way anyone could have known that I would take them!

Just calm down. You're getting paranoid.

Either way, Mr. Mike. Either way, you're paranoid.

So what choice do I have?

You have to *make* a choice.

One slow step at a time, I retraced my steps back onto the shore. When I turned, the raft had already begun its way back. Charon pushed the oar like clockwork, up and down, back and forth, further away.

Away, and the mist and fog swallowed—all I had left were the bells, but they were muffled. Muted. Unreal. Jeni playing her piano through the midnight walls, each door forever closed and locked between us.

No key.

Here on the opposite shore were fewer alternatives. Up and down the river-bank, the ground was reduced to spongy marshland.

I could go nowhere either way. What I did have were three open passageways, all silent. All dark but for the brief flicker of firelight somewhere within the middle cave. The bells were even softer now, further away on the opposite side of eternity.

Then almost… finally… gone.

Alone with the eerie red strobe and—

Do you remember?

Yes, I thought adamantly.

Do you really remember?

Damnit, already!

I remembered it all too clearly, another snippet from my past made real by this alien environment. My last year in college—walking across campus in the semi-gloom. Moira and I saw each other three times a day during the week: breakfast, lunch and lastly at midnight. We'd go either to her parent's house or mine on the weekends, but during the week we had our midnight rendezvous. We would meet outside her dorm, on the side of the building facing the hill the observatory sat upon.

A bench waited there; old-fashioned, cast-iron, full of character and unbelievably comfortable. We called it our "magic bench" for of all the time we spent there, we saw no one else. Heard no one else. We were magically invisible to all around us. The world could not touch us. Wouldn't dare!

A few weeks before winter break (then our senior year) I traversed the quad to the bench and sat there, waiting. I continually checked my watch. Ten after twelve. Fifteen after. When she walked through the side door, I watched her through a soft fall of snow. She stood there in the doorway, holding the door open. Near silence. My heartbeat. My breath. The light behind Moira was celestial, an aura of softness.

She would always walk over to me, to the bench covered by a wooden canopy, protecting it from the weather. Instead she smiled, standing there, holding the door open.

Behind her dormitory, I noticed a flash of red. To the right. Again—and I saw: the security lamp on a neighboring dorm was in the process of burning itself out. Stroboscopic flash-cube pops of cherry-red.

I looked away, rose from the bench and moved toward Moira. It was Friday evening and we planned to spend the weekend together. Wouldn't go home. Her room-mate left the afternoon before to visit her family in Ellsworth.

The snow melted between us as I neared, and melted all the more as I crossed the threshold of the open door.

The winter was not a cold thing, but a new and strange blanket that found me. Found us. It would follow us up two flights of stairs to room 211. I'd held her before, but had never until that next morning woken in her arms.

At that moment, *morning* was something in the far and distant future, an eventuality we could put off as long as we cared to.

As she opened her bedroom door, I smelled her washed hair and brushed the back of her neck with my lips.

Yet through all of this, I could not rid myself of the blood-red flash through the falling snow. A beacon.

A dark omen.

Still standing there on the moist lakeshore, before the middle passage.

A warning?

But why?

I hadn't thought of the light since that evening.

This new light flickered with greater insistence. Crazed from within the tunnel.

The breeze carried new scents...

I moved in closer, into the red strobe, touched the

sweaty rock of the middle cave's wall. Breathed deeper. It was there!

I wasn't imagining it!

The red light grew quicker still. I took my steps slowly—hand still pressed to the wall—and another scent joined that of the first. The air grew warmer.

Less damp.

My feet were caked with drying mud.

So this is where the water went, I thought. The rain that seemed to go nowhere. The rest was for our dreams and heart. What remained came here.

And waited, as I feared it would.

Another step and I found myself on firmer ground. Kneeling, I felt not sand nor mud, but carpet. This was the first smell: new carpet. Shedding my sneakers and socks, I continued along barefoot. The red light began to fade as a warmer, orange light took its place. A million miles above, muted thunder spoke a counterpoint to my silent step; concert-hall applause that bounced off everything. Rude and oblivious.

Still walking.

The second smell grew stronger, though I tried to push it away. It hurt!

Moira's baked chicken.

I tried to understand, but was so lost.

You're in Hell, buddy, torture's what it's all about. A bizarre thought: I never knew Hell had wall-to-wall carpeting.

The tunnel kept turning. Right. Then left. Left again. The red flashes were entirely gone now and the other light, though still faint, grew stronger; welcoming.

I felt exhausted and popped another capsule into my mouth. Swallowed. I don't remember if it all happened quickly or not, but at some point I was running. Not with any great speed, but fast enough.

I ran from the carpeted passageway into a room, my study from the house in New York. Everything was exactly as I had left it.

I stopped, stunned, then moved quickly to my desk, ran my fingers over the keys of my typewriter. *This* was my typewriter, not the impostor back in the empty house on Blackberry Way. This was the real one! With something you grew to know and understand with such intimacy, there was no room for question.

From beyond the walls, I listened to a television, muffled. And voices. Sweet voices that—

A radio... the living room stereo: "Take it Easy" by the Eagles.

Yet there weren't any doors, the only way in or out remained the hole back into the tunnel.

Thunder.

And rain, too!

No, just the river.

But it couldn't be the river. You left it far behind. This was different.

And it was true. This sound was something I knew well. Rain on the roof. On the house. On the windows. Everywhere.

A sheet of paper waited in the typewriter. I clicked the roller up a few notches and read:

HOME NOW LAST CHANCE TELL THE TRUTH TELL THE TRUTH TELL THE TRUTH

Difficult to stand. Harder to think. I moved toward the chair Moira had always sat in and eased myself down into it.

The music beyond grew louder.

TELL THE TRUTH

What truth? There wasn't any truth. Not now. Not ever.

The music advised: "Don't let the sound of your own wheels make you crazy..."

Chicken.

My mouth watered. The kitchen would be just down the hall, to the right, but there wasn't any *door!* No way out, except for—

Thunder.

Rain on the roof.

But there wasn't any roof! No outside. I'm not in a house! Can't be. I'm in Hell, miles buried.

Yet still I listened.

Tried to relax.

Closed my eyes.

Waited.

You want to know the truth?

Fine, then. Listen:

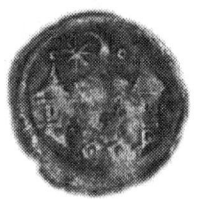

twenty-three

The truth is I wasn't as strong as I'd once believed. I always thought I was a fighter. That I could conquer any obstacle, master any problem.

The truth is, on my own, I was incomplete.

I could, however, be strong with my family. With Moira and Jeni, I had reason to be strong. I had a purpose in life.

Now I was nothing more than a living shell, wanting so much to give and to love, but incapable. Lost.

So why go on, Mr. Mike?

Leave me alone.

Why don't you just take the rest of the capsules? One at a time... all at once... end it all?

And the Eagles sang. And knocking. Knocking on a door that wasn't there and her voice, so sweet, yet strange, from beyond the walls that weren't.

"Michael? Are you okay?"

I held my eyes closed so tightly they hurt. Held my hands to my ears and hummed to block it all out. So afraid. Was this the final moment of complete mental breakdown? I could still hear her speaking to me over the hum.

I grabbed the cushion off the chair and pulled it over my ears.

Held it. Still, muffled:

"Michael? Are you alright?"

Baked chicken. Images, sounds and smells, all spinning madly. Wheel of misfortune.

"Michael?"

Why didn't she stop?

I ran from the chair and sat before the typewriter, stared at the keys swimming before me. Focusing wasn't easy, but I managed. I'd done it once before and it had worked. The trick had worked and everything was fine... at least for a while.

Crossing mental fingers, I typed, **STOP**

Waited.

"Michael? Are you..."

Typed it again: **STOP**

"...okay? Michael? Are you..."

STOPSTOPSTOPSTOPSTOPSTOPSTOPSTOPTOP

But it wouldn't.

And do you know why, Mr. Mike? Because this time it isn't a game from inside. This isn't one of your tricks. It's real. *Real.* I stared at this one word repeated. Last time it was so easy. I simply turned the madness off.

Stop complicating the world! Not everything has a hundred different meanings!

And just then the last capsule I'd taken kicked in. A static rush filled my body—I was already beginning to enjoy this feeling.

"Michael? Are you are youareyouareyou—?"

It was then that I began to notice things again.

Like the color of the wood paneling. Light brown. *Too* light. I remembered putting the paneling up myself, choosing the grain of wood. This wasn't it.

"—youareyouareyouareyou—?"

And the overhead light. There never was an overhead light in my study. Just the fisherman's lamp. I pulled the chair over and climbed up onto it. Upon closer inspection, I found something familiar. Through the base of the lighting fixture (which was transparent) watched the eye of a camera. The same "eye" that had been lurking in the restaurant as well as the trees.

"—areyouareyouare—?"

And a breeze that came not from the cave passage, but from somewhere in the room. A quick search revealed a vent concealed by a brown sheet of felt cloth matching the wood paneling. I peeled back the fabric and put my face to the fine steel mesh behind it. Through this vent blew the haunting smell of chicken.

TELL THE TRUTH

The truth? Was there such a thing? Or was the truth a lie with a different name?

"—areyou—?"

Am I what? Stupid?

I gripped the end of a section of paneling and pulled. Pulled hard. Open up said the world at the door.

Behind the artificial wall was a cross-sectioning of two-by-fours. And through the boards I spied a dim room, its only furnishing an enormous desk and swivel chair.

Louder:

"—AREYOUAREYOUAREYOU—?"

The room beyond was relatively empty. Walls of grey, painted cinder-block. The only other distinguishable features, aside from the desk and chair, were a small door and ladder. The door sat on the opposite side of the false room and the ladder rose upward into a dark aperture in the ceiling.

I wanted to yell, to scream.

"—AREYOUAREYOUAREYOU—?"

I kicked further through the wood frame and paneling and forced myself through the makeshift opening, squeezed past with splinters in my hair, scraping my arms and neck on raw wood, dust in my mouth, coughing, falling out onto the floor of the room beyond.

Solo delivery.

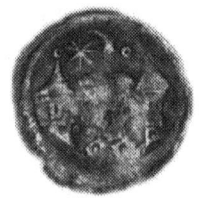

twenty-four

"—AREYOUAREYOUAREYOU—?"

I ripped the speaker from behind an exposed plank of wood and the words—as well as the rain on the roof—died instantly. The wire that trailed from it (almost completely hidden) went up the wall and into the ceiling just a few feet to the left of the ladder.

There was, of course, something waiting to replace this new silence.

Water.

Running water, but not that of a river, or stream, or storm. Different. I walked to the desk and discovered dozens of tiny black-and-white monitors embedded within it: a miniature studio. Beneath each screen were thin strips of tape with words written on them: *LIVING ROOM ENVIRONMENT, BEDROOM ENVIRONMENT, BACKYARD ENVIRONMENT, RESTAURANT ENVIRONMENT, RIVER BANK ENVIRONMENT...*

And so on.

Below these screens sat a larger monitor and keyboard, identical to those in Marsh's living room. A menu was currently displayed: *VOICE OVER A, VOICE OVER B, VOICE OVER C, OLFACT A, OLFACT B, OLFACT C, AUDIO (LOOP1), AUDIO (LOOP2), SUBLIM A (INIT), SUBLIM B, SUBLIM C (CATH SYNTH)*

And so on.

I chose from the menu *AUDIO (LOOP 1)* and from somewhere above came the faint sound of The Eagles.

I chose *OLFACT B* and smelled, faintly, baked chicken.

These: the strings which had controlled my life. To pull one needed only to tap a button. Run a program. My eyes ran over the screens. Standing where I was, I flew quickly through my house, Marsh's house, the front yard, back yard, down the hill and into the trails, into the cave, over the dead river and into Hell. I saw it all.

A sound from beyond the door behind me: the scraping of shoes on tile. In three quick steps I bolted to the door, both hands ready on the release bar and my ear pressed carefully against warm steel. The echo of footfalls, then silence.

Except for the Eagles above, and running water.

And don't forget that chicken.

Holding my breath, I pushed down on the bar and let the door click open on its own weight. When enough space allowed for a quick peek, I stared out into a sterile, white hallway; equally spaced doors and bluish-tinted lights in the ceiling were all that broke the monotony. The hall ran, endlessly it seemed, in both directions. The very moment I risked a step outside, a nearby door clicked open and I pulled my own door shut as quickly and quietly as I could manage. Looking down, I discovered a round, metal button on the handle. I pushed it in, hoping (praying) that I was locking it.

Putting my ear again to the door, I jumped back in terror as the unknown walker gripped the handle on the other side and pushed it down, then down again without success. I glanced around: the gaping hole in the wall where I'd escaped the false study, the desk, the ladder...

And still, from above, running water.

I had no where else to go but up. I had reached the lowest point possible. But I'd broken the dream! Shattered it. Behind the scenes now. Listening as, once again, footsteps faded (at a noticeably quicker pace) beyond the door.

I set my foot on the bottom rung of the ladder and took hold of another bar level with my chest. Looked up. Began my ascent. The rushing water was louder now, though still muffled, distorted.

Thunder too, but softer, less threatening, retreating.

I hoped for, but could see no light at all. The higher I climbed, the more rapidly the light retreated, and still louder: the water.

Softer, the thunder.

At the top of the ladder, I was borne once again through a membrane of darkness. I pulled myself up and rose to a standing position. Reaching out, I discovered walls on all sides, no more than a five foot stretch in each direction. Then I found a doorknob, turned it, and stepped out of Marsh's first floor hallway closet.

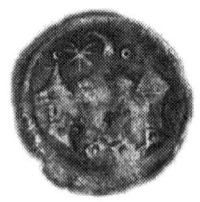

twenty-five

Pulsing waves of aqua. Sea-green undulations reflected organically on the walls. The air did not move. Another roll of thunder claimed the distance as I stepped into Marsh's living room. From the kitchen, I heard the sink still running with water, as I had left it. And, faintly, the click of a door.

The computers were still on, though each screen was blank. A dozen or so squares of ocean shade. The curtains were open and beyond I watched the sky. The final vestiges of daylight seeped through a fabric flaw in the retreating storm. It seemed as if I'd been down there an entire night, yet the darkness was a ruse. The clouds had brought it down prematurely. I watched as a three year old woken from a dream, finding hope in remembrance only through watery light. Glancing toward my own house, I watched a shadowy figure move quickly, disappearing through my front door. Though it was impossible to determine merely by sight, I knew who this shape belonged to; felt it, recognized it completely. I raised my line of sight higher...

The clouds flew with deliberate speed, leaving in their wake broken trails of smoke. And more light. Magically, the air seemed clean. And my mind, forced through the ringers time and again, washed over with thoughts pure and impure. I looked far and away and watched the trees, the wilderness. So very far away. Impossible to believe that I had been down there. Impossible that I was even here.

So? Here I am! And it's morning!

Except it wasn't *really* morning. It just seemed like it. Almost night, this time for real.

But the light—

Yes, the light...

I started again toward the hallway, noticing a blip on each of the monitors. I hesitated a moment, but kept moving. Pretended not to see.

But I did see: one word floating in so many blue-green fields:

HOME

And it really was home, wasn't it? Home, where I wanted so much to be. Home, where there was no more home. And I left the house with this word. Whispered it. Kept it with me.

Standing on the front porch, I watched it all. The breeze was post-storm and clean and full of washed leaves. From beyond fell the rich tone of a bell. Not that of the raft, nor the impostor who commanded it; different. Entirely different. As sweet as Jeni's toy piano, yet different still. A distant church, and there was nothing evil about it. A true and pure sound.

A sound like home. There: I could hear it well now, sense it, but had no idea where it was. No idea where anything was. Still barefoot, I left Marsh's lair and walked toward my house, toes collecting loose clay and weed on the way. I didn't bother trying to scrape it off. It felt good there.

The distant bell now completely replaced the thunder; it grew no louder, no softer. Merely tolling invisible hours, not counting, not caring, just there. Not an artificial sound, nor a facade. It was an integral part of the landscape.

I pondered the sky a bit longer. The satellite dishes at the top of Marsh's hill were silent, unmoving. No information flying.

I reached into my pocket and recovered the remaining capsules. One by one, I pushed them from the foil packaging and cupped them in my hand. About thirty, like tiny opalescent stones washed fine and smooth by time and wind. And water. Always water. Their shiny coats caught the sky and broke the heavens into a myriad puzzle of similar tales. I felt I knew them all by heart, the same story told so many different ways, though still the same with no way out. There was no way to physically change a story already written without re-writing it.

This was law.

So where could I possibly go? I was trapped in a place so horrible, so demanding and unfair that I was beyond fear or hope. I had written these prisons for a living, devising characters who were eventually doomed. Doomed not by me, but by their final chapter. Their epilogue. From the very first word until the last, they acted out their part and that was it. Can't go back and change things. Can't start from scratch. On and on until the pages ran out.

Exactly where I had been caught I didn't really know. Perhaps at the very beginning. The day I told Moira I loved her? Jeni's birth? The day I learned they were dead? When did it all begin?

Impossible questions, I know, but aren't all questions impossible? Some are difficult and some utterly simple, but in the end not one single answer can ever hold the permanence of truth.

The flicker of what at first seemed like a flame, yet

wasn't. Looking up, I found the glow in the window, where I knew it must be. The master bedroom window. I put the capsules back into my pocket and thought about Marsh. The way he had always looked at me. His eyes. Knowing, yet not knowing. Searching.

The sky filled for long seconds with the bright, artificial breath of daylight.

And then it went dark. The afterglow assumed the outline of the house and surrounding trees and strange thoughts. Thoughts that whirled mindless circles. But that's secondary. The light, no matter how much I wished, would never come back to the heavens.

And I could never turn back the pages. Never change the words. Only watch the glow from above...

HOME

...and move helplessly toward it.

twenty-six

We held hands.

Our first date was strange in that we didn't *know* it was our first date. It was nearing the end of the day, toward the trail-end of October. The air was quick-chilled and my jacket would soon be replaced by a heavy, down-lined parka. We happened to be at the same place at the same time, so we walked. Simple as that. Walked all over. Walked to the observatory hill and sat there watching the autumn leaves in the dusk. We told stories, sitting side by side, in almost the same place Pete and I had sat the afternoon I received his first sermon. And the sky grew colder and the day turned out its light. We moved a little closer, looked into each others eyes, and we held hands...

I stepped up to the house and found the front door wide open. Dim light defined only vaguely what waited within. I stood there in the doorway, waiting.

twenty-seven

We held hands.

After we'd made love for the very first time, hidden in the cool reaches of her bedroom at school, snow coating the world beyond. Speaking only in perfect whispers, holding one another, vowing never to let go. We'd found what we were searching for. There was no need to reach further. Right there before us...

And I moved into the empty living room. No furniture. No smells. No tricks. No need for it. I stopped, finally, at the kitchen door. It was closed. A thin rime of light spilled from the top and bottom.

My days in this strange place were innumerable years strung out before me on a thread of blind hope. Not faith, for such a thing was as impossibly frail and delicate as the truth, but hope.

Beyond the door a collision of worlds, and I was not

afraid; who's afraid of the big bad wolf? Beyond the door a way of facing the darkness (once and for all) that ultimately waited beyond any light. Beyond all light.

Beyond *my* light.

twenty-eight

We held hands.

In marriage, I placed the ring on her finger and promised to give her all she had given me from the very beginning. We were one. Inseparable.

We spoke that evening (drifting off to sleep for the first time as husband and wife) of our wedding. Of how we had been married long before. A marriage before the traditional ceremony. A marriage unspoken as two people walk with one another, not having to say a thing, knowing each other well enough to allow for speech without words. Holding hands...

My hand on the kitchen door, the wood neither hot nor cold. Merely wood. Just a door.

I pushed it open and the sink, as in Marsh's house, was still on and offering. Wading through a shallow ocean, I turned the tap off. Silence.

The light over the stove was on and that was it, the rest shadows, and in them a voice. I passed into the dining room and stared at the darkness within the dark.

"Michael?" it asked. The thunder returned, barking at the edges of reality... I said nothing.

Waited.

Heat lightning through the window to my right and a snapshot of Peter, his face grave, sitting at the head of the table. I waited for him to repeat my name.

He didn't.

"I made it," I told him flatly.

I was speaking to darkness, but the lightning seized in shorter bursts as time passed. I wondered idly if this lightning was manufactured, not part of the natural world, of mechanical or mental effect.

"Tell the truth," I said, unable to stop shaking.

Lightning.

I caught him smiling sadly.

Shifting my weight from one foot to the other, I whispered, "Are you through playing games, Pete?"

Thunder.

But hadn't the storm left? Weren't the clouds moving away when I last looked?

"Are you finished playing with my life? With everything?" My voice was gaining force, and it took an equal amount of will to hold it back. I took a breath.

Quieter, I asked, "Are you?"

Lightning.

He was now standing, face intense, stare icy, jaw firmly set. With the next strobe of light, however, I watched his stoic veneer melt, his lips loosen, mouth drag slowly open.

"It's done, Michael. I'm through." Sitting again, he leaned forward on the table and nestled his head in the space between his crossed arms.

His voice muffled, "I didn't mean for it to happen this way. It wasn't supposed to go this far with you."

"What are you talking about," I asked.

"Last night Moira convinced me to end it all. To stop this insanity." He lifted his head a moment, "She really loves you. I'm convinced of that now. I..."

Reduced to tears, my oldest friend provided the rain. The thunder drew ever closer, each silvery wash of lightning an all preserving snapshot, each sob a dream of hopeless expectancy; we were dark, orphaned clouds painted in harsh strokes on an artist's unclean canvas.

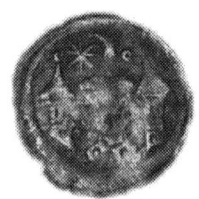

twenty-nine

We held hands.

In the delivery room. I knew the day was nearing, but it forever seemed a point in the future. Now it was there before us both. Her body bathed in sweat, the air antiseptic. Moira squeezed my hand and I watched her eyes. I gave her all the strength I could offer. Though I had once thought that nothing could possibly make us stronger than we already were, it was a wonderful surprise to discover how much closer we had grown after Jeni was born. Each part of our lives took on added dimensions. Sitting quietly in the living room, reading a book, Moira going over her schedule re-assignment for work, Jeni dozing quietly in her bassinet at the center of the room... simple things that made me cherish what I had, made me all the more glad to be alive...

My voice was dry and I barely managed: "You spoke with Moira last night?" I was afraid if I spoke any louder my world would fall again to ashes.

Pete stood slowly, resigning himself to a straighter, though no less sure posture. His voice was thin:

"She's the one who made me see that what I did was wrong."

Lightning.

"What did you do?"

He spoke cautiously, not meeting my eyes. "There never was a car accident, Michael. But I needed the lie to get you down here. I've been working for years with others, though I've never told you much about that. I won't be specific now, but this goes way beyond what I started out doing. The government has been involved for the past eight years. Data of this nature is as valuable as any bomb or mechanical device. More to the point, you've become an invaluable asset. I've tried to keep you to myself and out of their immediate line of sight, but I was foolish."

He was pacing back and forth now, reverting back to his just-sit-back-and-I'll-explain-everything mode.

Thunder.

"I wanted only one thing," he continued, "They wanted it all."

They. I thought back on the nearing footsteps in the hallway far below. Were *they* coming as we now stood there in the dining room? I tried to focus, fighting for balance between blind hatred and my eternal hope.

"What did you want?" my voice fought to be tight, though raced out of control. Bright, liquid taps on the window behind him broke into short-lived prismatic worlds as the sky again filled with ever-increasing electricity. I watched Pete's face as it dissolved further of any evil, real or imagined.

The bass grind of thunder.

The soft whisper of rain.

"You, Michael," and his voice was not his own, "It's always been you, but you never saw. When Moira came along I thought I'd lose you. I thought that... she'd hurt you. I couldn't have that, so I waited. I knew deep inside that one day we could be together. That you'd see... we'd..."

Again falling into the chair behind the table, I watched him struggle. He appeared on the verge of speech again, though couldn't manage more than warbled, incoherent syllables.

"My God!" I croaked, my throat constricting; I understood exactly what he was saying. I suppose I knew it all along, but wasn't able to accept it. Still... Moira alive...?

"I didn't mean for it to come to this. I only wanted you to be happy and to—"

"Moira!" I shouted, "You said you talked with her?"

His tears flowed again, voice angry, "It's all my fault. I used the Swiss facility without telling them, but I never thought they'd see what I was up to. I never thought—"

"Where's my family!" I screamed, ignoring a hundred other questions that ravaged my mind, contemplating this one last possibility. In a frenzy, I leaped forward, skirting the edge of the table and grabbed him roughly by the shoulders.

"Where are they!" I demanded.

"Gone," he said with a hollow sound.

Letting go, all I could do was stare.

"After I spoke with Moira last night, they lethally injected her. Jeni, too. They overheard our conversation. You have to believe me, Michael. I was going to stop this. I was going to try and get you out of here. All three of you."

That same heavy, tired, overwhelming misery filled my veins yet again.

"Why haven't they killed me then?" I asked, wishing the act had already been committed.

Pete's voice thickened, "You're too important. The first complete success. Total immersion with complete external control. The power they have... you just can't comprehend..."

I looked up at him sharply. *I* couldn't comprehend? I was the one led to believe that my backyard was the Underworld!

A dark point waited before me, growing larger as the

seconds passed. Darkness without rules or judgment. Encroaching oblivion. I felt Pete's hand gently rest upon my lowered head and recoiled back in disgust, allowing a burning hatred to rise again inside me. I stood quickly.

"How dare you touch me," my words were acid, "You took my life from me. You took everything."

"Not everything," in a voice near inaudible.

"What could I possibly have left?" I was aghast. Then I saw his eyes. I

"You think that I could...? How could you possibly think that I'd accept you? You've torn me to pieces and left nothing."

A sound from outside. The down-shifting of gears, the whine of an engine.

"They're here," Pete said, "Go upstairs."

I looked at him questioningly, then jumped as I heard the slam of a car door, or perhaps a van door. My heart skipped spasmodically in my chest with frantic abandon.

"Go!" he shouted, and I ran.

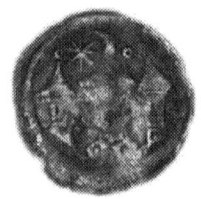

thirty

We held hands.

Moira, Jeni and I in the late afternoon, two days after Jeni's fifth birthday, the final week in September. I held Jeni's left hand and Moira her right and we walked a clear path at the far northern end of Harriman State Park. We drove to the park after an early dinner, singing along with Billy Joel on the car stereo. Jeni tried her best to emulate the chorus of "Piano Man" as we walked along. Everything was fine. Things couldn't have been better. I was with the two people whom I loved more than anything and would do anything for. The bond was there and nothing could ever break it.

Even now.

The master bedroom was as bare as I had last left it, save for one thing. Off to the right sat the canopy bed. The artificial light from the fixture above hurt my eyes, burned them, so I threw the switch and saw the room only in what dim illumination filtered through from downstairs.

And there was the lightning, too.

I walked slowly toward the bed.

More lightning.

Taking a deep breath… holding it… they were there on the bed, eyes open, unmoving. Not destroyed in a car accident, beyond recognition. Not buried in New York.

Rain on the window.

I dove into my left pocket and pulled out the remaining blue capsules. In several swallows I took them all. From my right pocket I recovered the remaining two coins. Felt the weight of them in my hand.

Kneeling at the side of the bed, I watched them. Moira's cheeks were bone white. Cold. And Jeni...

Let out my breath. Explosive.

I could stop the tears (the real tears) for only so long; I gently placed one obol past Jeni's lips. The other was for Moira. I'd already used mine, had already passed over, though knew that such a fate was not part of their destiny. I placed the coins in respect. I did so because there was nothing left for me to do, hoping only that wherever they were, they had one another.

Thunder.

For this was all Pete had left me. I listened distantly as the front door opened below. Footsteps. Voices. As the seconds passed, however, the footsteps did not find me. Was Pete stalling them? Allowing me this final time with my family? Postponing the inevitable? Whatever the reason, there was nothing left. Without my wife and daughter, I had nothing. What else was there? A life at the mercy of cold psychologists? Of icy, government manipulation? Forever at the mercy of drugged-induced mind-alteration and subordination. This, surely, was no life.

I carefully crawled into bed between them, thinking one last time about the truth. The more I thought, the more I decided there really was some truth after all. A small truth, perhaps, though as large as the love I held for my lost angels.

I closed my eyes and took hold of each of their hands. In reality, their fingers were cold and lifeless, unreciprocating, yet in my mind I could feel their warmth, their beating hearts, and it was a good thing. I thought of all the wonderful times we shared together, and this was also good.

And I knew that love was undying and traveled all realms, passing between them with perfect ease.

The seconds passed slowly and soon I could no longer see the silvery flash of lightning through closed eyes. Could no longer hear the roll of thunder. Could only hear the gentle rain, and the words that followed me here, to this room, grateful for their existence. Three words that held the only truth I could unconditionally believe in, unconditionally accept:

We held hands.

afterward

Michael did not mention when or where he wrote his journal entries. I would guess that he probably wrote in the evening, though it could easily have been accomplished at random intervals given the erratic nature of the writing.

Now here are a few somewhat disturbing facts I have unearthed. The first is, perhaps, the most startling. Michael Dorigan never married. There was no Moira and no Jeni. If one believes the narrative and further accepts the near total control Pete had over Michael, then the absence of a prior family augments the power of this horrific manipulation. It also brings into question how early Pete had begun seeding Michael with information. Perhaps as early as their college years?

Pete, unlike Michael's fictional family, was very real. Looking back into Michael's past, I discovered that nearly everything he mentioned about Pete was true. I visited the

University of Maine at Orono. I toured the campus and even walked through Michael's old dormitory, Oxford Hall. I stood on the steps outside the observatory, closed my eyes and imagined that Michael and Pete were talking nearby. It was all incredibly surreal.

Also, Michael was not a novelist, though he did take creative writing courses while in school. He did not know his birth parents and spent years in a state institution before being adopted at the age of seven by an older couple. There is no mention of a sister named Rose, adopted or otherwise.

After Pete received his doctorate in psychology, his trail all but completely disappeared. Pete Fausta's name appeared only fleetingly, though was linked to several respected institutions, including the Department of Experimental Psychology at Oxford, Cambridge and Cornell. I even uncovered evidence that he once consulted for the American government through *DARPA, Defense Advanced Research Projects Agency. DARPA* officially denies any association with someone named Peter Fausta.

There is a small river behind my new home, about two hundred feet into the pine forest. Standing out there, I can almost lose myself in Michael's fantasy. Still, I have not yet found an entrance to any sort of underground passage. Each time I wander the property, I scan the ground, hoping to find one of the small speakers or transmitters. The house that supposedly belonged to Marsh (according to the real estate agent) burned down years ago and has since been replaced by another home, set further back from the cul-de-sac and down a lengthy driveway. Whoever lives there now values their privacy. I have not yet met them.

Other items: I could find absolutely nothing relating to Marsh. He is quite an enigma. Was he a fabrication as well, or another victim? If only I had his last name…

Most of the signs mentioned in the notebooks, including the names *Sweetwater*, *La Vista* and *Weatherstone*, are gone. The name of the street I live on, however, is still called *Blackberry Way*.

For a while, I thought Tiny Peco's restaurant was fictional as well, but stumbled accidentally upon a woman named Tekki who claimed to be his sister. According to her, after Peco's wife passed away (food poisoning, she explained) Peco moved to New Mexico and died a year later of pneumonia.

It's as if Michael's entire account happened in some alternate reality.

Part of me shudders to think that an experiment utilizing such extreme methods of subliminal persuasion and mind control could actually have occurred, but I am not so naïve to dismiss all of it that easily. I constantly ask myself the same question whenever doubt settles in: *why were the notebooks hidden in the wall?*

There is still so much yet to explore and uncover. The further I reach, however, the colder the trail becomes. It is my hope that someone will read this and bridge some connection I have missed. There is no solid record of what might have happened to Michael Dorigan or Pete, but I have not yet given up.

Part of me wonders if Michael might be out there this very moment. What if he was only led to believe that he was about to die? So many questions... It's only a matter of how much deeper I have to dig to answer them.

Walter Klimczak grew up in the Catskill region of New York State and majored in English at the University of Georgia. He lives with his wife and three children in Atlanta, Georgia. He is the author of *Falling in the Garden* and *This Place Only*, the first two novels in the TimeFront series.